François-René
de Chateaubriand

Vicomte François-René de Chateaubriand, born at Saint-Malo in 1768, spent his boyhood in the Breton peninsula in an atmosphere permeated with Celtic myth and folklore. In 1791 he obtained through the statesman Malesherbes a commission to seek out the Northwest Passage. During the five months he spent in America he became fascinated with the American Indian and the American landscape. On his return to France Chateaubriand married Céleste Buisson de la Vigne. He joined the Armée des émigrés and was wounded at the seige of Thionville in 1792. He went to England in 1793 and during his seven-year stay he wrote his first sketches for *Atala* and *René*. Both of these stories were incorporated in *The Genius of Christianity* which was published in 1802. This work was a brilliant success, partly because Napoleon was restoring Catholicism as the state religion, and as a reward, Napoleon appointed Chateaubriand secretary of the legation to Rome. The following year, 1804, Chateaubriand became an anti-Bonapartist and resigned his post. After 1815, his royalist writings brought him several diplomatic appointments; he abandoned the diplomatic field in 1830. In addition to those books mentioned, his most important works are *The Natchez* (1826) and *Memoirs from Beyond the Tomb* (1849–50). Chateaubriand died in 1848.

François-René de Chateaubriand

ATALA & RENÉ

A NEW TRANSLATION WITH
A FOREWORD BY *Walter J. Cobb*

A SIGNET CLASSIC
Published by THE NEW AMERICAN LIBRARY

First Printing, January, 1962

SIGNET CLASSICS *are published by*
The New American Library of World Literature, Inc.
501 Madison Avenue, New York 22, New York

PRINTED IN THE UNITED STATES OF AMERICA

O3901

Foreword

François-René de Chateaubriand was born at Saint Malo, September 4, 1768. His youth—melancholy, sad, and lonely—was spent in or near this city by the sea. Educated at the Collège of Dol, Rennes, and then at Dinan, where his classical studies were terminated, he dreamed of adventures at sea, or thought about entering the priesthood. At seventeen he went to live with his parents at their château in Combourg, a few miles northwest of Rennes. The austere reserve of his father ("One passion possessed my father—name"), the warm piety of his sickly mother ("As for her piety, my mother was an angel"), and the nervous, quixotic nature of his sister, Lucile ("No one could have suspected that in poor, sickly Lucile such talents and beauty would one day shine.") had much influence on his personality. From his father, Chateaubriand derived his pride; from his mother, his mysticism and imagination; from Lucile, his sense of classical beauty. The dark surrounding woods of Combourg,

the resounding solitudes in the vast chambers and isolated towers of the château itself, the music of the
near-by sea—all these elements by some inexplicable
alchemy combined to form Chateaubriand, the man
and writer. "These waves, these winds, this solitude,"
he wrote, "were my first masters."

At twenty, he entered the army, intent upon win-
ning fame and fortune in distant lands, but the Revolution changed his plans. In 1791, with his father dead
and his regiment disbanded, he obtained through Malesherbes a commission to explore the Northwest Passage, an expedition that took him, according to his
own inaccurate account, on extensive journeys on the
Great Lakes and over the vast savannahs of America,
from the upper reaches of the Hudson to the tropics
of Florida. Thus, for a period of five months, he was
brought into contact with Rousseau-like Indian "children of nature." They afforded him opportunities to
indulge his soul in the poetry of these primeval forests.
From these peregrinations were born all his future
works, especially *Les Natchez*, conceived at this time,
though it was to remain unpublished for more than
thirty years. *Atala* (1801) and *René* (1802) owe their
origins to Chateaubriand's sojourn in America. These
were originally two episodes connected to *Les Natchez*.

The debauches of the Revolution, specifically the
Reign of Terror, revamped Chateaubriand's political
ideals of reform; and on his return to Europe (1791),
he married Céleste Buisson de la Vigne hastily and un-
happily, to suit the whims of his forward-looking
parents. He joined the Armée des émigrés, was
wounded at the siege of Thionville (September, 1792),
and finally, in 1793 went to England, where for seven
years as an exile he supported himself by tutoring and
translating literary work. It was in England that he

wrote his *Essai sur les révolutions*, a pessimistic and skeptical tour de force against human progress and Christianity. "What did I hope to prove in the *Essai?* That there is nothing new under the sun and that we find in all revolutions, past and present, the characters and principal traits of the French Revolution." In England, too, he made his first sketches of *Atala, René,* and *Les Natchez*—all three infused with the spirit of Bernardin de Saint-Pierre's *Paul et Virginie* and Rousseau's *Émile.* These three works display a marked change in Cheaubriand's religious attitudes, which to this point had been free and unorthodox, the typical posture of eighteenth-century philosophy. This change was effected, he tells us, by his grief at the deaths of his mother (May, 1798) and sister, Mme. de Farcy (July, 1798). "I wept and I believed." Henceforward, he was to write in defense of religion. It was his way of expiating his sins against the faith in which he had been raised.

Chateaubriand returned to France in 1800. The following year he published *Atala*, which was a universal and immediate success, making of Chateaubriand the lion of literary circles. "The publication of *Atala* dates the reputation I have made for myself in this world . . . . It is then my public career began." In 1802 he published the *Génie du Christianisme* and it, too, was a brilliant success, due in large part to Napoleon's Concordat (July 15, 1801), which reconciled France and the Catholic Church.

Unquestionably, Chateaubriand was now the leading light in French letters and remained so till the appearance of Lamartine's *Meditations* (1810).

The *Génie du Christianisme* ushered in a new kind of Christian apologetics, which eighteenth-century philosophers ridiculed and severely attacked. It represented a new base on which to rest a philosophy of criticism and aesthetics. The author of the *Génie* was less interested to find Christianity *true* than to find it sentimentally poetic and aesthetic. The first title Chateaubriand gave to his book is significant: *Beautés morales et poétiques du Christianisme*.

Chateaubriand, whose exaltation of Christianity meshed with Napoleon's plans, received a diplomatic post in Rome (1803). He was involved in a great number of intrigues, was transferred to Switzerland, and on the execution of the Duke of Enghien (1804), resigned his post and began a critical campaign against Napoleon, who, he said, "made the world tremble, but me—never!"

In 1806, after his rupture with Napoleon, he began an extensive journey, visiting Greece, Turkey, Asia Minor, Palestine, Tunis, and Spain. He wrote of his impressions in *Les Martyrs* (1809), a prose epic of rising Christianity and sinking paganism. He wrote *Itinéraire de Paris à Jérusalem* in 1811 and *Les aventures du dernier Abencérage* in 1826. The fall of Napoleon inspired *De Buonaparte et des Bourbons* (1814), which, according to Louis XVIII, was worth 100,000 men to the Legitimist cause. The work brought its author several diplomatic appointments, which he resigned in order to be free to oppose the ministries that displeased him; and around 1830 he seemed tending toward liberalism. The Orléanist triumph brought him back promptly to the lost cause. Chateaubriand now sank into a discouraged silence. He translated *Paradise Lost* (1936), wrote a *Vie de Rancé*, (1844), and revised and completed his *Mémoires d'outre-tombe*, first published in France in the years 1849-1850.

He is buried in Saint Malo, on the island of the Grand Bé, facing the sea, alone, isolated, as he wanted to be. "I shall rest finally by the seaside which I have loved so much."

There have been few books in the history of French literature which, upon first publication, have appealed so universally and instantaneously as did *Atala*. There have been few books, indeed, which have so refreshingly responded to the need of their times as did Chateaubriand's little volume when it appeared in 1801. It immediately brought the public to gaze upon a brilliant new star, hitherto obscure, in the literary heavens —a lodestar that illuminated and maneuvered a revolutionary movement in French letters: romanticism. Within months of its publication, new editions, translations, fraudulent imitations followed one another in rapid succession. Chactas, Atala and Père Aubry inspired playwrights, painters, and makers of wax dolls; they nettled the die-hard "philosophers" and elicited from their pens venomous, mocking sarcasm. But while the old guard fumed and ranted, a new century was dawning over the horizon, and a new generation with a youthful, vigorous spirit went to meet Chateaubriand to usher in the day.

Sainte-Beuve wrote in his *Portraits Littéraires:* "Every man endowed with great faculties, and living at a time when they have an opening for revealing themselves, is responsible before his century and before humanity for the production of a work in harmony with the general needs of the age and tributary to the march of progress." To this "sacred law of genius," Chateaubriand answered with *Atala*.

The needs of the age did cry certainly for a recharging of the wellsprings of art. Individualism, imagination, feeling, and religion had not only been neglected, they had been suppressed and condemned by the age of reason. The literature of the first half of

the eighteenth century was impersonal, didactic, phil-
osophical, and, for too long a time, dedicated to the
rules of good sense and reason. Philosophers and
French writers were too intent in their search for
truth, too one-sidedly bent on finding man's place
in the universe. Reason and scrupulous analysis were
the salient characteristics of the era. Man's rational
nature and his behavior in society were minutely ex-
amined, dissected, and analyzed. Christianity came under close scrutiny and severe attack. It was ridiculed
and rebuffed. Literature in France, devoid of heart,
emotional appeal, and a feeling for nature, was char-
acterized by the all-too-classic style of Voltaire.

In the second half of the century the ramparts of
reason began to crumble. The French public began to
weary of the dry, analytical, proselytizing philosophers. It turned eagerly to other literatures and was
charmed by new influences. The novels of Richard-
son and Fielding, with their elaborate descriptions of
the familiar and even seamy sides of life, the poetry
of Gray, Macpherson, and Ossian—very popular in
France at this time—and Goethe's *Werther*, which between 1776 and 1797 went through fifteen editions in
France, created a new climate for lyricism, personality, emotion, and mystery to explode and become the
fashion in French letters. Buffon, because he revealed
to the French public "the true majesty of nature,"
Diderot, because he taught "the expansive virtue of
enthusiasm," and especially Rousseau, because he ex-
tolled the delirium of imagination and the delights of
sentimentality—were all exceedingly popular as they
rode on the crest of the surging tide of romanticism.
The time was right; Chataubriand arrived on the scene.

Atala and *René* contain all the essential elements of
the newborn romantic movement, a movement that
was to live until 1850. It is impossible to appreciate

French literature of the period without an understanding of the principles at work in these two short
works of Chateaubriand.

Atala and *René* were originally destined as chapters
to appear in *Les Natchez,* an epic poem-novel which
Chateaubriand had conceived during his stay in America and had composed, at least partially, during his
first stay in England. But when he left London in
1800 to return to France, he left behind this volumi-
nous manuscript, excepting these two episodes, in-
tending to insert them in a monumental work, *Génie
du Christianisme. Atala* would serve to demonstrate
"the harmonies of the Christian religion with the
scenes of nature and the passions of the human heart";
René would illustrate the terrible consequences of
impassioned love and solitude, and the efficacy of
religion to heal our wounds.

The plan of *Atala* is classically delineated: prologue,
narrative, and epilogue. The narrative is made up of
four parts: The Hunters, The Tillers of the Soil, The
Drama, The Funeral. Chateaubriand intended *Atala*
to celebrate the intrinsic value and beauty of the
Christian religion, the highest law of man. Hence we
find implicitly within the framework of a rather
simple love story, artistically told, a social and religious message. Human nature is bad, civilized man is
corrupt, religion is necessary to control and restrain
his passions. In the person of *Atala,* the natural law
and the Christian law meet head-on in a war "to-the-
death." The indecisive yearning of Chactas for the
"vie sauvage," the regrets of Lopez, Père Aubry's
glorification of the pastoral life tempered by reason
emphasize the tensions and concerns of the new
century in its quest for new dimensions in literature and art.

René is to France what *Werther* was to Germany and *Childe Harold* to England. All three planted the the seeds of melancholy which infected the literature of the early nineteenth century and diseased the body of all Europe with the "*mal du siècle.*" The established type of the "homme fatal" was René. His is a nature of insatiable desires which reality fails to satisfy. His is a nature of morbid yearnings, interminable brooding, unbridled emotions. René's is an egocentric nature. He lives out his life, refusing to compromise his individuality and solitude, and dies tragically.

René was the first of a long line of introspective, disoriented, pessimistic heroes, characteristic of romantic literature.

Chateaubriand gave new direction to imagination and principles of literary criticism. His style, rhythmic and harmonious, left its mark on fiction, poetry, and the language itself. With Chateaubriand a new dawn was breaking.

ATALA

Prologue

At one time France possessed a vast empire in North
America, extending from Labrador to the Floridas,
from the Atlantic coast line to the most interior regions of the lake district of upper Canada.

Four large rivers have their source in the mountains
of this empire and divide these immense regions: The
St. Lawrence River in the east empties into the Gulf
of the same name; the West River carries its waters to
seas unknown; the Bourbon River rushes from south
to north into the Hudson Bay, and the Mississippi
flows from north to south into the Gulf of Mexico.

This last-mentioned river, running its course of
more than a thousand leagues, waters a delightfully
beautiful country, called by the people of the United
States the New Eden, and named by the French,
musically, Louisiana. A thousand other rivers, tri-
butaries of the Mississippi—the Missouri, the Illinois,
the Arkansas, the Ohio, the Wabash, the Tennessee—
nourish the land with their silt and fertilize it with
their waters. When all these rivers by winter's thaw

are at flood stage, when storms have felled whole sections of forests, uprooted trees clog the streams. Soon the sludge cements them, the bindweed chains them, and plants taking root all over them, finish by matting this debris. Borne along by the frothy waves, they are swept down to the Mississippi. The great river seizes them, carries them to the Gulf of Mexico, casts them upon sandy shores, and thus the mouths of the river are increased. Intermittently, its voice is heard, passing by the mountains along the river banks, and washing its flooded waters around the stately colonnades of the forest and pyramids of Indian tombs. It is the Nile of this wilderness. But grace is always welded to splendor in nature's scenes: while the middle current sweeps the dead pines and oaks to the sea, one can see, on the side currents, floating isles of pistia and water lilies, whose pinkish yellow flowers, rising like little banners, are carried along the river banks. Green serpents, blue herons, pink flamingoes, young crocodiles sail like passengers on the flower-ships, and the colony, unfolding its golden sails to the wind, lazily drifts into some hidden bend of the river.

The two banks of the Mississippi present a most unusual picture. On the western bank, savannahs range until they are lost from view; their green billows, going off in the distance, seem to meet the blue of the sky, where they disappear. On these limitless prairies can be seen herds of three or four thousand wild buffalo wandering around at random. Sometimes a lumbering old bison, furrowing through the waves, comes to rest in the high grass on some island of the Mississippi. The two crescents adorning his forehead and his shaggy, muddy beard suggest some god of the river complacently overlooking the grandeur of his waters and the wild abundance of his shores.

Such is the scene on the western bank, but it changes

on the opposite side, and forms a striking contrast to it. Suspended above these waters, clumped together on rocks and mountains, scattered in the valleys, trees of all shapes, of every color, of all odors, blend, growing side by side and rising to heights which weary our vision. Wild vines, trumpet flowers, and colocynths entwine the base of these trees, scale the boughs and climb to the ends of the branches. They jump from the maple to the tulip tree, from the tulip to the marsh mallow, forming a thousand grottoes, a thousand arches, and a thousand porticoes. Often wandering from tree to tree, these vines make floral bridges across the arms of the river. From the heart of these clusters of trees, the magnolia raises its unwavering cone; topped by its large pinkish-white blooms, it overlooks the entire forest, and has no other rival but the palm tree, which ever so gracefully beside it waves its green fans.

A large number of animals, placed by the hand of the Creator in these solitudes, add enchantment and life. At the ends of avenues one can see bears drunk with grapes unsteady on the branches of the elm trees; caribou bathe in the lake; black squirrels caper in the thick foliage; mocking birds, Virginia doves bigger than the sparrow, alight on the grass red with strawberries; green parrots with yellow heads, purple woodpeckers, and fire-red cardinals move to the top of the cypress trees; hummingbirds sparkle on the jasmine of the Floridas. Bird-catching snakes hiss, suspended from the domes of the forest, and swing back and forth like the vines.

If all is silence and repose in the savannahs, on the other side of the river everything is, on the contrary, sound and movement: peckings against the trunks of oak trees, hustlings of animals walking about, grazing or cracking nuts with their teeth, the babbling of brooks, weak moans, muffled cries, and gentle cooings

—fill these forest spaces with a wild, sweet harmony. But should a breeze happen to quicken these solitudes, to rock these floating bodies, to confuse these masses of white, blue, green, and pink, to mix all these colors, to combine all these murmurings, then there arises from the depths of the forest such sounds and there passes before the eyes such sights that I would in vain try to describe them to those who have never traveled these primeval fields of nature.

After the discovery of the Mississippi by Père Marquette and the unfortunate La Salle, the first Frenchmen who settled in Biloxi and New Orleans made a pact with the Natchez, an Indian nation whose power was formidable in these parts. Quarrels and jealousies afterward bloodied this hospitable land. Among those savages there was an old man named Chactas who, by age, wisdom, and knowledge of life, was the patriarch and the beloved of the wilderness. Like all men, he had achieved his stature through suffering. Not only were the forests of the New World filled with his sorrows, but he had borne them to the shores of France. He was held prisoner in Marseilles by a cruel stroke of injustice. Then he was given his freedom and later presented to Louis XIV. During his life he spoke with the great men of this century, attended the Court functions at Versailles, was present at the tragedies of Racine and the funeral orations of Bossuet. In a word, this savage had seen the splendor of society from the highest vantage point.

After he returned to his native country, Chactas enjoyed repose for several years. Nevertheless he paid heaven dearly for this favor; the old man became blind. A young girl accompanied him over the hills of the Mississippi, as Antigone guided the steps of Oedipus over Cithaeron, and as Malvina led Ossian over the rock of Morven.

In spite of the countless injustices which Chactas had experienced at the hands of the French, he still loved them. He always remembered Fénelon, whose guest he had once been, and he wished he could render some service to the compatriots of this virtuous man. In 1725, a Frenchman named René, driven by his passions and sorrows, arrived in Louisiana. He traveled up the Mississippi as far as the land of the Natchez, and asked to be considered as a warrior by this nation. Chactas quizzed him, found him resolute in his determination, adopted him as his son, and gave him in matrimony an Indian named Celuta. A short time after their marriage, the Indians prepared for the beaver hunt.

Chactas, though blind, was designated by a council of sachems to command this expedition because of the respect in which he was held by the Indian tribes. Prayers and fasting began; the medicine men interpreted dreams, the Manitou was consulted; sacrifices of tobacco were made; the tongues of elks were burned. These burnings were closely observed to see if they crackled in the flames, in order that the will of the spirits might be discovered. Finally they departed for the hunt, having partaken of the sacred dog. René was a member of the group. With the help of countercurrents, the canoes went up the Mississippi and entered the mouth of the Ohio. It was autumn. The magnificent wilds of Kentucky lay before the astonished eyes of the young Frenchman. One night, by moonglow, while all the Natchez slept in their canoes and the Indian fleet, with its sails of animal skins still raised, was drifting with a light breeze, René remained alone with Chactas and asked him to relate the story of his adventures. The old man consented, and sitting down beside him in the stern of the canoe, began in these words:

The Tale

THE HUNTERS

It is a strange fate, my dear son, by which you and I are drawn together. I see in you the civilized man who has become a savage; you see in me the savage man whom the Great Spirit (I know not why), has wished to civilize. Having both entered life's course by opposite ends, you have come to rest in my place and I have sat in yours; thus our outlooks should be totally different. Who, you or I, has gained or lost the most by this change of station? The spirits know, and the least wise of them has more wisdom than all men together.

At the next moon of flowers, it will be seven times ten snows and three snows more that my mother brought me into the world along the banks of the Mississippi. The Spanish had been for a short time settled in the bay of Pensacola; but no white man lived as yet in Louisiana. I had barely seen the falling of leaves seventeen times when I marched with my father, the warrior Outalissi, against the Muskogees, a powerful nation in the Floridas. We joined ourselves as allies with the Spaniards and battled on one of the branches of the Mobile River. Areskoui and the Manitou were not favorable to our cause. The enemy triumphed; my father lost his life; and defending him I was twice wounded. Oh, if I could have then descended into hell, I would have avoided all the sorrows that were attending me on earth. But the spirits ordained it otherwise; with the refugees I was shunted along to Saint Augustine.

In that city, newly built by the Spaniards, I ran the risk of being whisked away to the mines of Mexico, but an old Castilian called Lopez, who was touched by my youth and simplicity, offered me a refuge and introduced me to his sister with whom he lived without a wife.

Both grew very fond of me. They reared me with much care, they furnished me with all kinds of teachers. But, after thirty moons in Saint Augustine, I developed a strong distaste for city life. Plainly I was wasting away. Sometimes for hours I remained motionless, gazing at the summit of the faraway mountains; sometimes they would find me on the bank of a river, sadly watching it flow. I would picture to myself the woods through which these waters had passed, and my soul would be entirely steeped in solitude.

No longer able to resist the pull of the wilderness, one morning I betook myself to Lopez, garbed in my Indian skins, holding my bow and arrows in one hand and my European clothes in the other. I returned them to my generous protector, at whose feet I prostrated myself, shedding torrents of tears. I leveled against myself hateful names; I accused myself of ingratitude. But at last I said to him, "Oh good father, you see for yourself; I will die if I do not live my Indian life again."

Lopez, overcome with surprise, wished to turn me from my resolution. He told me of the perils I would encounter, falling once more into the hands of the Muskogees. But seeing my determination to undertake all, he pressed me in his arms, weeping: "Go," he said, "child of nature! Be an independent man. This I would not rob you of. If I were younger, I would go with you into the wilds—I too have pleasant memories of that life—and I would return you to the arms of your mother. When you are in the forests, be mindful sometimes of this old Spaniard who was hospitable to you. Remember that you may be brought to love your fellow man, that your first experience with the human heart was all in its favor." Lopez finished with a prayer to the God of the Christians, whose religion I had refused to embrace, and we parted with tears and sobs.

My ingratitude was soon punished. Through inexperience I lost my way in the wood and a tribe of Muskogees and Seminoles captured me, just as Lopez had predicted. I was taken for a Natchez by my dress and the feathers that adorned my head. They tied me, but loosely, on account of my youth. Simaghan, chief of the band, wanted to know my name. I answered, "I am called Chactas, son of Outalissi, son of Miscou, who bore away more than a hundred scalps of Muskogee heroes."

Simaghan said to me, "Chactas, son of Outalissi, son of Miscou, rejoice; you shall be burned in the big village."

"Very well," I answered, and I intoned my death chant.

Prisoner though I was, during the first days I could not help but admire my enemies. The Muskogee—and also his partner, the Seminole—is all gaiety, affection, and contentment. His step is light, his manner is forthright and serene. He speaks much and fluently; his speech is harmonious and smooth. Even age cannot take from the sachems this joyous simplicity. Like the birds in our woods grown old, they blend their ancient songs with the new melodies of their young offspring.

The women who accompanied the band treated me, because of my age, with tender pity and affectionate curiosity. They questioned me about my mother, about my earliest years; they wished to know if I had been suspended in my cradle of moss from the flowery branches of the maple tree, if the breezes rocked me to sleep by some nest of little birds. Then there were a thousand other questions about my heart's desires: they asked if I had ever seen in my dreams a white doe, and if the trees in some secret valley had counseled me to love. I replied naïvely to these mothers, and daughters, and wives of these men. I said to them, "You are the delight of the day, and the night loves you like dew. Man leaves your womb to cling to your breast and to your lips; you know magical words to lull all our sorrows to sleep. This is what I have been told by her who brought me into the world, whom I shall see no more. She told me, too, young maidens were strange flowers found in solitary places."

These praises very much pleased the women. They showered me with all kinds of gifts: nut cream, maple sugar, corn meal, bear hams, beaver skins, shells with which to deck myself, and moss for my bed. They sang and laughed with me and then, remembering that I was to be burned, they began to shed tears.

One night when the Muskogees had camped on the edge of the forest, I was seated near the war fire with the hunter charged to guard me. Suddenly I heard the rustle of clothing in the grass, and a woman, half-veiled, came and sat beside me. Tears streamed from her eyes; by the light of the fire a small crucifix of gold gleamed on her breast. She was beautiful, with even features. On her face one could detect a certain virtuous, passionate air the charm of which it was impossible to resist. Joined to this there were more tender charms. Extreme sensitivity and profound melancholy shone through her eyes; her smile was from heaven.

I thought it was the *Maiden of Last Loves* sent to a war prisoner to charm his final hours. Thinking this, I said to her, stammering and with much difficulty, though I had no fears of the stake, "Maiden, you are worthy of a first love, you were not destined for the last. Sentiments of the heart about to cease beating can only respond weakly to yours. How can life and death be fused? You would make me too much regret the day. Let another be happier than I. Let the vine and the oak entwine with long embraces!"

Then the young damsel said to me, "I am not the *Maiden of Last Loves*. Are you Christian?"

I answered that I had not betrayed the spirits of my cabin. At these words the Indian girl was startled. She said to me, "I am sorry for you, sorry that you are only a wicked heathen. My mother made me a Christian. I am called Atala, daughter of Simaghan of the Golden Bracelets, and chief of the warriors of this band. We are returning to Apalachucla, where you shall be burned." Saying these words, Atala rose and departed.

At this point Chactas was constrained to interrupt his tale. Too many memories filled his mind. From his sightless eyes tears poured down his wrinkled cheeks. Like two hidden springs whose waters filter through the rocks in the dark night of the earth, his eyes were betrayed by their tears.

O my son, he began again, you see how little wisdom I have, in spite of my reputation. Alas, my dear child, even though men can no longer see, still they can weep! Several days passed and the daughter of the sachem came back each evening to speak with me. Sleep had fled my eyes, and Atala was always on my mind, like the memory of my parents' love.

On the seventeenth day of the march, about the time when the day fly leaves the water, we entered the great Alachua plain. It was enclosed by hills which, stretching back of one another and rising into the clouds, seem to carry with them the liquidambars, lemon trees, magnolias, and green oaks. The chief gave the cry of arrival, and the band camped at the foot of the hills. I was brought to a spot a little distance away, on one of the edges of these natural wells so famous in the Floridas. I was tied to the bottom of a tree, and one of the warriors guarded me impatiently. I had scarcely spent a few moments in this spot when Atala made her appearance under the liquidambars at the fountain. "Hunter," she said to the Muskogee hero, "If you wish to chase the roebuck, I will guard the prisoner." At these words from the daughter of the chief, the warrior was overjoyed. He bolted down from the summit of the hill and sped in the direction of the plain.

How strangely contradictory is the heart of man! I who had so wanted to reveal my secret feeling to her whom I already loved like the sun, was now thwarted and confused. I think I would have preferred being thrown to the crocodiles in the stream than to have found myself alone thus with Atala. This daughter of the wilderness was as troubled as her prisoner.

We kept a long silence; the spirits of love had robbed us of speech. At last Atala made an effort and spoke thus: "Warrior, you are loosely tied; you could escape easily." At these words, boldness came back to my tongue and I replied, "Loosely tied, O woman . . . !" I could not finish. Atala, hesitating a few moments, said, "Flee!" And she untied me from the trunk of the tree. I took the cord; I put it into the hands of this strange daughter, forcing her to close her beautiful fingers around my chains.

"Take them! Take them!" I cried.

"You know not what you are doing," said Atala in a voice indicative of her feelings. "Unfortunate one! Don't you know you will be burned? What do you want? Do you not know that I am the daughter of a formidable sachem?"

Tearfully, I cried, "There was a time when I was borne in a beaver's skin on the shoulders of my mother. My father too had a fine hut, and his roebucks drank the waters of a thousand streams; but now I am a wanderer without country. When I shall be no more, no friend will cover my body with grass to protect it from the flies. The body of an unfortunate stranger interests no one."

Atala was saddened by these words. Her tears fell into the fountain.

"Ah," I continued, quickened, "would that your heart spoke out as mine! Is not the wilderness free? Have not the forests corners where we might hide? For their happiness, do children of the cabins need so much? O daughter, more comely than the husband's first dream! O my beloved, dare to follow me." Such were my words.

Atala answered tenderly, "My young friend, you have mastered the language of the white man. It is easy to deceive an Indian girl."

"What's this?" I exclaimed. "You call me your young friend! Ah! If a poor slave . . . !"

"Well, then," she said, bending toward me, "if a poor slave . . ."

I began again ardently: "Let a kiss assure him of your trust."

Atala heard my prayer. As a fawn seems to cling to the flowers of the pink lianas, taking them with its delicate tongue from the steep slopes of the mountains, thus I remained clinging to the lips of my beloved.

Alas, my dear son, our sorrows are near pleasures. Who would have believed that the moment when Atala gave me the first pledge of her love would be the very moment when she would smash all my hopes? Whitened hair of old Chactas, what was your astonishment when the daughter of the sachem pronounced these words:

"Handsome prisoner, I have foolishly given in to your desire; but where shall this passion lead us? My religion will always separate me from you . . . O my mother! What have you done?"

Suddenly Atala was silent, guarding in her heart I know not what fatal secret about to fall from her lips. Her words plunged me into despair.

"Well," I exclaimed, "I shall be cruel like you; I will not run away. You shall see me in the fire, you shall hear the hissing of my skin, and you shall be filled with joy."

Atala took my hands into hers. "Poor young heathen," she cried, "how I pity you! Do you wish my heart to bleed? What a pity 'tis that I cannot flee with you! Unfortunate, O Atala, was the womb of my mother! Why do I not throw myself to the crocodiles?"

At that very moment, since the sunset was approaching, the crocodiles began to make their noises. Atala said to me, "Let us leave these parts." I led the daughter of Simaghan to the foot of the hills, which formed verdant gulfs, projecting their promontories over the savannah. All was calm and magnificent in the wilderness. The stork was crying from its nest, the woods echoed the monotonous song of the quail, the whistling of parrots, the bellowing of bisons, and the neighing of Seminole mares.

Our walk was a silent walk. I walked beside my Atala; she held the end of the cord which I had made her take again. Sometimes we cried, sometimes we tried to smile. Sometimes looking heavenward, sometimes looking down, an ear attentive to the song of birds, a gesture toward the setting sun; a hand tenderly squeezed, a breast palpitating, then calm, the names of Chactas and Atala sweetly repeated at intervals . . . . O first walk of love, your memory must be powerful indeed, since, after so many years of misfortune, you still stir the heart of old Chactas.

How incomprehensible are men stirred by passion! I had just quitted kind Lopez; I had just exposed myself to all sorts of dangers in order to be free; in an instant a woman's glance had changed my tastes, my resolutions, my thoughts! Forgetful of my country, my mother, my cabin, and the terrible death awaiting me, I had become indifferent to all which did not concern Atala! Without strength to reason like a man, of a sudden I had regressed to a kind of childishness; and far from being able to do anything that might save me from the misfortunes awaiting me, I was almost in need of someone to look after my sleeping and eating.

So it was in vain that after our wanderings in the savannah, Atala, prostrate at my feet, again asked me to leave her. I firmly refused, saying that I would return alone to the camp, or return with her so that she could bind me again to the foot of my tree. She was obliged to accede to my wishes, hoping to persuade me another time.

On the day after this, which decided my life's destiny, we stopped in a valley, not far from Cuscowilla, capital of the Seminoles. These Indians with the Muskogees form the confederacy of the Creeks. The daughter of the country of palm trees came looking for me in the middle of the night. She led me to a large forest of pine trees and implored me once again to escape. I did not answer, but took her hand in mine and forced this doe to wander about the forest with me. The night was delightful. The Spirit of the Air was shaking its blue locks, perfumed with the smell of pines, and we breathed the languid odors of ambergris which the crocodiles exhaled while sleeping under the tamarinds of the river. A moon shone in the cloudless heavens and its pearl-gray light fell on the limitless summit of the forests. No sounds were heard except those distant in the depths of the forest. One could say that the soul of solitude was sighing through the expanse of the wilderness.

We noticed through the trees a young brave, holding in his hand a torch, who was like the Spirit of Spring wandering in the forests breathing life into nature. It was a lover who was going to the cabin of his mistress in order to learn his fate.

If the maiden puts out the torch, she accepts his proposal; if she veils herself without extinguishing it, then she refuses a husband.

The warrior, stealing through the shadows, was softly singing:

> "I shall outdistance the steps of the day to the summit of the mountain, to look for my solitary dove among the oaks of the forest.

"I have draped around her neck a necklace of shells; with three red beads for my love, three purple ones for my fears, three blue ones for my hopes.

"Mila has eyes of ermine and hair soft like a field of rice; her mouth is a pink shell, studded with pearls; her breasts are like two spotless kids, born of a single mother on a single day.

"May Mila extinguish this torch; may her mouth cast over it her voluptuous shadow! I shall make fertile her womb. The hope of a country shall cling to her heavy breasts, and I shall smoke the pipe of peace over the cradle of my son!

"Ah, let me outdistance the steps of the day to the summit of the mountain, to look for my solitary dove among the oaks of the forests."

Thus sang this young man, whose accents pierced even to the depths of my soul, and changed the expression on Atala's face. Our joined hands trembled. But we were distracted from this scene to another no less ominous for us.

We passed the tomb of an infant, which served as a boundary line for two nations. It was placed along the edge of the road, according to custom, so that the young women on their way to the fountain might attract to their bosoms the soul of the innocent creature and return it to the fatherland. We saw at this moment two newly married girls who, yearning for the sweetness of motherhood, with lips parted, were striving to suck in the soul of the child whom they imagined they saw wandering in fields of flowers. Then its real mother came to place a sheaf of corn and some lily blossoms on the grave. She watered the earth with her milk, sat on the wet grass and spoke to the child tenderly:

"Why do I mourn for you in your cradle of earth, O my newborn? When the little bird becomes big, it must look for its food, and it finds it in the wild bitter seeds. At least you have not known sadness; at least your heart has never been bared to man's destructive breath. The bud which dries up in its encasement passes away with all its perfumes, like you, with all your innocence, O my son! Happy are those who die in the cradle: they have known only the kisses and smiles of a mother."

Already subdued in our own hearts, we were overwhelmed by these images of love and motherhood, which seemed to pursue us through these enchanted, lonely places. I carried Atala in my arms into the depths of the forest, and I told her things that today I would seek in vain to find on my lips. The south wind, my dear son, loses its warmth passing over icy mountains.

In the heart of an old man, memories of love are like day fires reflected by the peaceful orb of the moon, when the sun has set and silence hovers over the huts of the Indians.

Who could save Atala? Who could prevent her from being charmed by nature? Nothing but a miracle, no doubt, and that miracle happened! The daughter of Simaghan had recourse to the God of the Christians. She threw herself on the ground and prayed fervently to her mother and the Queen of Virgins. From this moment, O René, I have stood in awe of this religion, which in the forest, amidst all the privations of life, can shower upon the wretched a thousand gifts. I have marveled at this religion which, opposing its might against the torrent of passions, alone is enough to conquer them when everything favors them: the secret of the woods, the absence of men, and the faithfulness of shadows. Ah! How divine she seemed to me, this simple savage, this ignorant Atala, kneeling before an old fallen pine, as at the foot of an altar, offering to her God prayers for the heathen lover! Her eyes, lifted toward the night star, her cheeks, shining wet with tears, with religious fervor, and with love, were all immortally beautiful. Several times it seemed she would take flight into the heavens, several times I thought I saw descending on the moon's rays and on the limbs of the trees, these spirits whom the Christian God sends to hermits of the rocks, when He is about to summon them unto Himself. I was grieved, for I feared Atala had but a short while on this earth.

However, she wept so many tears, she was so distraught, that perhaps I was about to consent to leave her when a cry of death echoed through the forest. Four armed men came rushing toward me; our flight had been discovered and the war chief had been given the order to pursue us.

Atala, who was like a queen in her proud bearing, disdained to speak to these warriors. She glanced at them haughtily and returned to Simaghan.

She could obtain no favors. They doubled my guards, they multiplied my chains, they took away my beloved. Five nights passed, and we caught sight of Apalachucla, situated on the banks of the Chattahoochee River. Immediately they crowned me with flowers, they painted my face blue and vermilion, they hung pearls on my nose and ears, and they placed in my hand a chichikoué.

Thus decked for the sacrifice, I entered Apalachucla. Repeated cries were raised from the crowd. My fate was determined when suddenly a blast from the conch was heard, and the Mico, or chief of the nation, ordered an assembly to be held.

You know, my son, the tortures to which savages subjected their prisoners of war. Christian missionaries, at the risk of their lives and with tireless charity, succeeded, with several nations, in substituting a rather

mild form of bondage for the horrors of the stake.
The Muskogees had not yet adopted this custom, but
a great number had declared themselves in favor of it.
It was to pronounce on this important matter that the
Mico had convened the sachems. They led me to the
place of their deliberations.

Not far from Apalachucla, on an isolated hillock,
rose a council pavilion. Three circles of columns
formed the elegant architecture of this rotunda. The
columns were of cypress, polished and carved; they
increased in height and thickness and diminished in
number as they approached the center, which was
marked by a single pillar. From the top of this pillar
bands of bark jutted out and passed over the top of
the other pillars, covering the pavilion in the form
of an opened fan.

The council assembled. Fifty old men, garbed in
beaver, arranged themselves in tiers facing the door
of the pavilion. The grand chief was seated in the
middle of the assembly, holding in his hand a peace
pipe scarcely half-colored for war. To the right of
these old men were fifty women robed in dresses of
swan feathers. The war chiefs, tomahawks in hand
and plumage on head, arms and chests painted with
blood, were to the left of the assembled group.

At the base of the central column burned the fire
of the council. The first medicine man, surrounded
by eight guards, dressed in long robes and wearing
a stuffed owl on his head, poured balm from the
liquidambar into the fire and offered sacrifices to the
sun. This triple row of old men, matrons, and warriors,
these priests, these clouds of incense, this sacrifice, all
served to add pomp to this assembly.

I was standing in chains in the middle of the assembly. When the sacrifice was finished, the Mico spoke
and explained quite simply the question before the

assembly. He threw a blue necklace, a symbol of peace, into the hall, in testimony of what he had just said.

Then a sachem of the Eagle tribe arose and spoke: "My father the Mico, sachems, matrons, warriors of the four tribes of Eagle, Beaver, Serpent and Turtle, let us change nothing of the customs of our ancestors; let us burn the prisoner; let our courage be not soft. It is a white man's custom that is proposed; it can only be injurious. Give the red necklace, symbol of war, which contains my words. I have spoken."

And he threw into the midst of the assembly the red necklace.

A matron rose and spoke: "My father Eagle, you have the mind of a fox and the slow prudence of a turtle. I would polish the chain of friendship with you and we shall plant together the tree of peace. But let us change the customs of our forefathers if they are evil. Let us have slaves to cultivate our fields and no more let us hear the wailings of prisoners which haunt the breasts of our mothers. I have spoken."

Like the waves of the sea that swell during a storm, like the dry leaves of autumn that are swept away by gusts, like the reeds of the Mississippi that bend and straighten in a sudden flood, like a great herd of deer that bell in the depths of the forest, so did the council stir and murmur. Sachems, warriors, matrons spoke in turn or all together. Interests clashed, opinions were divided, the council was about to break up, but finally the ancient custom triumphed and I was condemned to the stake.

One circumstance delayed my punishment, the *Feast of the Dead* or *Festival of Souls* was approaching. During the days consecrated to these ceremonies, it is the custom not to put any captive to death.

They entrusted me to a strict guard; and undoubtedly the sachems took the daughter of Simaghan away, for I saw her no more.

In the meantime, nations for more than three hundred leagues around arrived in large numbers to celebrate the *Festival of Souls*.

A hut in a remote spot was constructed. On a designated day, in each cabin, the occupants exhumed the remains of their fathers from their tombs, and they hung the skeletons, by rank and family, on the walls of the *Community Room for Ancestors*. The winds—a tempest had arisen—the forests, and the waterfalls roared outside, while the old men of the various nations concluded between them treaties of peace and alliance over the bones of their forefathers.

They celebrated the funeral games, races, games of ball, and knuckles. Two young girls tried to get from each other willow sticks. The buds of their breasts touched, their hands moved up and down the willow branch which they raised over their heads. Their pretty bare feet locked, their mouths met, their sweet breath mingled, they bent over and their hair meshed; they looked at their mothers, blushed, and all applauded. The medicine man called upon Michabou, the spirit of waters. He told of the wars of the Great Hare against Matchimanitou, god of evil. He told of the first man and of Atahensic, the first woman, fallen from heaven for having lost their innocence; of the earth reddened by their fraternal blood; of Jouskeka, the ungodly, immolating Tahouistsaron, the just one; of the deluge coming by the command of the Great Spirit; of Massou saved alone in his bark canoe and of the raven sent out to discover the land. He told too of the beautiful Endae, brought back from the land of the dead by the sweet chants of her husband.

After these games and hymns, they prepared to give their ancestors an eternal burial.

On the banks of the Chattahoochee River, a wild fig tree grew, worshiped by these people. The young maidens had been accustomed to washing their robes of bark at this spot and to leaving them to dry in the warm wind, hanging on the limbs of this ancient tree. It was there that they had dug an enormous grave. They left the funeral room, singing their hymns of death, each family carrying some sacred remains. They arrived at the grave, they interred the relics; they spread them out in layers, separating them with bear and beaver skins. A tombstone was raised, and they planted the *Tree of Tears and Sleep*.

Let us pity men, my dear son! These same Indians whose customs are so moving; these same women who had displayed such tender interest in me, now with loud cries were asking for my torture. Entire nations delayed their departure so they could have the pleasure of seeing a young man suffer excruciating torments.

In a valley, northward and some distance from the large village, there was a wood of cypress and pine trees, called the *Wood of Blood*. You arrived there through the ruins of one of these monuments whose origin and architect are unknown. In the center of this wood there was an arena in which prisoners of war were sacrificed. They led me there triumphantly. Everything had been prepared for my death. They planted the stake of Areskoui; the pines, the elms, the cypresses fell under the ax; the stake was readied; the spectators built amphitheaters out of branches and tree trunks. Each invented a torture: one suggested scalping me; another, burning my eyes with hot axes. I began my song of death.

"I fear not your torments. I am brave, O Muskogees, I defy you and despise you more than the women. My father Outalissi, son of Miscou, has drunk from the skull of your most renowned warriors; you will not get even a sigh from my lips."

Aroused by my song, a warrior stuck my arm with an arrow; I said, "Brother, thank you."

In spite of the activity of the executioners, the preparations for my torments could not be finished before sunset. They consulted with the medicine man, who forbade troubling the spirits of the shadows, and my death was put off until the following day. But in their impatience to enjoy the spectacle and to be all ready at daybreak, the Indians did not leave the *Wood of Blood*. They lighted large torches and began their celebrations and dances.

Meanwhile, they stretched me on my back. They passed cords around my neck, feet, and arms and secured me to stakes driven into the ground. Warriors were asleep on these ropes and I could not move without alerting them. The night waxed on. Gradually the songs and dances ceased; the fires only cast a reddish glow in front of which one could make out the passing shadows of some Indians. Everyone slept. As the noises of men died away, those of the wilderness grew louder, and above these noises could be heard the moaning of the wind in the forest.

It was the hour when a young Indian who has just become a mother is startled in the middle of the night because she imagines she hears the cries of her first-born asking for her sweet milk. With eyes fixed on the heavens, where the crescent moon was wandering in the clouds, I thought of my destiny. Atala seemed to me a monster of ingratitude. To forsake me in my moment of trial—I, who would have thrown myself to the flames rather than abandon her! And yet I felt that I would always love her and that I would die joyfully for her.

As in extreme pleasures there is a spur which awakens us as if to warn us to take advantage of these short moments, in great sorrows, on the contrary, I know not what heaviness puts us to sleep. Nature tries to close eyes tired from weeping, and the goodness of God is thus revealed even in our misfortunes. I yielded, in spite of myself, to this heavy sleep which sometimes the wretched enjoy. I dreamed that my chains were removed. I thought that I felt the relief which is experienced when, having been tightly bound, a helpful hand loosens our irons.

This sensation was so intense that I opened my eyelids. By the light of the moon, a shaft of whose light came between two clouds, I caught sight of a tall figure bending over me and busily and silently untying my bonds. I was about to cry out, when a hand which I recognized instantly closed my mouth. One cord remained, but it seemed impossible to cut it, without touching the warrior who covered it entirely with his body. Atala placed her hand on it; the warrior stirred drowsily and sat up. Atala remained motionless, and watched him. The Indian thought he saw the Spirit of the Ruins; he went back to sleep, invoking his Manitou. The bond was broken. I got up. I followed my liberator, who extended to me the end of a bow which she was holding by the other end. But what dangers encompassed us! Sometimes we almost bumped into sleeping Indians; sometimes a guard questioned us, and Atala would answer, disguising her voice. Children cried, watchdogs barked. Scarcely had we left this evil enclosure when howlings shook the forest. The camp was awakened, a thousand fires were lighted. We saw running every which way Indians with torches in their hands; we quickened our pace.

When dawn rose over the Appalachians, we had already gone a great distance. How happy I was to enjoy once more solitude with Atala, with Atala my liberator, with Atala who was giving herself to me forever! Words failed me. I fell to my knees and said to the daughter of Simaghan, "Men are indeed of little account, but when the spirits possess them, they are nothing at all. You are a spirit; you have visited me, and I am speechless before you."

Atala grasped my hand with a smile and said, "I must follow after you, since you will not flee without me. This night I wooed the medicine man with gifts. I made your executioners drunk with fire water, and had to risk my life for you, since you had given yours for me. Yes, young heathen," she said in tones which frightened me, "the sacrifice will be mutual."

Atala furnished me with weapons she had taken care to bring with her; then she bandaged my wound. Wiping it with a leaf of papaya, she moistened it with her tears. "It is ointment," I said to her, "with which you cover my wound."

"I fear rather that it is a poison," she replied. Tearing a piece of cloth from her bosom, with which she made a first compress, she made it fast with a lock of her hair.

Drunkenness, which lasts a long time with Indians and which for them is a kind of sickness, undoubtedly prevented them from taking chase after us those first days. If afterward they looked for us, it was probably to the west, convinced that we would have tried to reach the Mississippi. But we had followed our course in the direction of the fixed star, guiding ourselves by the moss on the tree trunks.

We were not slow to realize that we had gained little by my escape. The wilderness now spread its unbounded solitude before us. Inexperienced in the life of the forests, turned aside from our path, and walking around aimlessly, what was to happen to us? Often looking at Atala, I remembered the ancient story of Agar, which Lopez had made me read. That tale transpired in the wilderness of Beersheba long ago, when men lived three times the age of the oak tree.

Since I was almost naked, Atala made me a cloak from the second bark of the ash tree. She embroidered for me moccasins of muskrat with the hair of the porcupine. In turn, I adorned her. Sometimes I crowned her head with blue mallows, which we found in abandoned Indian cemeteries along the way. Sometimes I would make for her necklaces from the red seeds of the azalea bush, and then I would smile, gazing upon her exquisite beauty.

When we came upon a river, we crossed it on a raft or we swam. Atala would place one hand on my shoulder, and, like two traveling swans, we would sail these lonely waves.

Often when the day was very warm, we sought shelter under the moss on the cedar tree. Almost all the trees of Florida, especially the cedar and the live oak, are covered with a white moss which hangs from their branches to the ground. When at night, by moonlight, you see an isolated holm oak on the bare expanse of the savannah, draped with this dress, you would think you saw a phantom dragging behind it its long robes. The scene is no less picturesque by day, for a swarm of butterflies, brilliantly colored flies, hummingbirds, green parakeets, and bluejays come and attach themselves to this moss and produce an effect of a white woolen tapestry embroidered by a European artisan with insects and brightly colored birds.

It was in these festive hostelries, prepared by the Great Spirit, that we would rest in the shade. When winds came from the sky to sway this huge cedar, when this aerial castle built on its branches would undulate with bird-travelers asleep in its shelter, when a thousand sighs rose from these corridors and vaults of this moving edifice—never did the marvels of the Ancient World approach this monument in the wilderness.

Each night we lit a fire and constructed a hut of bark raised on four stakes. Whenever I killed a wild turkey, a wood pigeon, or a wild pheasant, we hung it over a burning oak at the end of a long pole driven into the ground and we let the wind turn the game of our hunting. We ate mosses called rock tripe, the sweet bark of the birch and the May apples, which have a peach and raspberry taste. The black walnut, the maple, and the sumac furnished the wines of our table. Sometimes I would go look among the reeds for a plant whose elongated bloom in the shape of a horn contained a glass of the purest dew. We gave thanks to Providence which, on this delicate stem of a flower, had placed this liquid spring in the midst of fetid marshes; just as He has placed hope in the recesses of a man's heart, ulcerated by grief, just as He causes virtue to leap from the bosom of life's miseries.

Alas! I soon discovered that I was mistaken about Atala's outward calm. As we went on, she became sad. Often she trembled without cause and turned around suddenly. I surprised her as she cast me an impassioned glance, and then looked heavenward with a profound melancholy. What especially frightened me was a secret, a hidden thought, deep in her soul, which I divined in her eyes. Always drawing me to her and then shunning me, always enkindling my hopes, then dousing them. When I thought I had made a little impression on her heart, I found myself where I had begun. How many times did she say to me, "O my young lover! I love you as I love the wooded shade at noontime. You are handsome like the wilderness with all its flowers and breezes. When I bend toward you, I tremble; when my hand falls in yours, I am ready to die. The other day when the wind blew your hair in my face, and you rested upon my breast, I thought I felt lightly the touch of the invisible spirits. Yes, I have seen the young goats of the mountains of Oconee, and I have heard the words of old men; but the sweetness of the kids and the wisdom of the wise men are less pleasant and less reassuring than your words. Ah poor Chactas, I shall never be your wife!"

The perpetual conflicts of Atala's love and religion, the abandonment of her tenderness, the purity of her conduct, the proudness of her character, her deep sensitivity, the loftiness of her soul in matters important, her delicateness in matters of small importance—everything made her an incomprehensible being. Atala's influence over a man could not be small: full of passions, she was full of power; you had either to adore her or to hate her.

After fifteen nights of rapid march, we entered the chain of the Allegheny Mountains and reached one of the branches of the Tennessee River, which flows into the Ohio. Advised by Atala, I built a canoe which I coated with the gum from the plum tree, sewing the barks together with roots of fir trees. Then I embarked with Atala, and we let ourselves drift with the current of the river.

The Indian village of Sticoe, with its pyramidal tombs and ruined huts, appeared on our left at a bend around a promontory. We passed on our right the valley of Keowe, at the end of which we could see the cabins of Jore, clinging to the brow of a mountain known by the same name. The river which was carrying us along flowed between high cliffs on the top of which we took note of the setting sun. These deep solitudes were not disturbed by the presence of men. We saw only an Indian hunter, who, resting on his bow and motionless on the top of a rock, looked like a statue raised in the mountain to the spirit of these wilds.

Atala and I joined our silence to the silence of this scene. Suddenly the daughter of exile shattered the air with a voice full of emotion and melancholy; she sang of her faraway fatherland:

"Happy are they who have not seen the smoke of the stranger's celebrations and who sit only at the festivities of their fathers!

"If the bluejay of the Mississippi said to the finch of the Floridas, 'Why do you weep so sadly? Have you not here beautiful waters, refreshing shades, and seeds of every kind as in your forests?' 'Yes,' would reply the finch, 'but my nest is in the jasmine. Who will bring it to me? And the sun of my prairie, do you have that?'

"Happy are they who have not seen the smoke of the stranger's celebrations, and who sit only at the festivities of their fathers!

"After difficult hours of marching the traveler sits down sadly. He contemplates about him the rooftops of men, the wanderer has no place where he may rest his head. He knocks at the cabin, he puts his bow behind the door, and asks for hospitality. The master of the house gestures with his hand, and the stranger takes his bow and goes back to his wilderness!

"Happy are they who have not seen the smoke of the stranger's celebrations and who sit only at the festivities of their fathers!

"Wonderful stories told around the hearths, tender outpourings of the heart, long habits of loving so necessary to life, you have filled the days of those who have never quitted the country of their birth. Their graves are in their country with the setting sun, the tears of their friends, and the charms of their religion.

"Happy are they who have not seen the smoke of the stranger's celebrations, and who sit only at the festivities of their fathers!"

So sang Atala. Nothing had interrupted her song except the soft sounds of our canoe slipping through the waves. In two or three spots alone they were picked up by a faint echo which repeated them to another fainter still, and then to a third even yet fainter. We could have believed that the souls of two lovers, once unblest as we, charmed by this touching melody, took pleasure in sighing its last laments in the mountains.

Meanwhile, the solitude, the constant presence of the beloved, our sorrows even, heightened our love with every moment. Atala's strength began to wane, and the passions, destroying her body, were triumphing over her virtue. She prayed constantly to her mother, whose wrathful shade she seemed to be appeasing. Sometimes she would ask me whether I heard a plaintive voice, whether or not I saw flames arising out of the earth. As for me, oppressed by fatigue, but always burning with desire, thinking I was perhaps lost in these forests never to return, a hundred times I was ready to seize her in my arms; a hundred times I suggested that we build a hut on these river banks and entomb ourselves there forever and ever. But she resisted always.

"Remember," she would say to me, "a warrior owes himself to his country. What is a woman beside the duties you must fulfill? Take courage, son of Outalissi, rebel not against your fate. The heart of man is like the surge of a river, which sometimes swells with muddy waters when the sky has troubled them. Has the river the right to say, 'I thought there would be no storms and the sun would never be burning hot'?"

O René, if you fear affections of the heart, beware of solitude. Great passions are solitary, and when you take them into the wilderness, you bring them to their natural home. Overwhelmed by cares and fears, exposed to the dangers of falling into the hands of enemy Indians, of being swallowed up by waters, of being bitten by serpents or devoured by beasts, of finding our poor nourishment only with much difficulty, and not knowing in which way to direct our steps, it seemed to us our misfortunes could not increase, when an accident brought them to a climax.

It was the twenty-seventh sun since our departure from the cabins: the *moon of fire* had begun its course and everything announced a storm. About the time when Indian matrons hang their plow sticks on the branches of juniper, and when the parakeets retire to the hollow of the cypress, the sky became overcast. Voices of the solitude were heard no more, the wilderness was all silent, and the forests enjoyed a universal calm. Soon the rumbling of the distant thunder, reverberating in the woods as old as the world, produced from its depths sublime music. Afraid of being drenched, we hastened to the river bank to take refuge in the forest.

The spot where we landed was marshy. We made our way with much difficulty under an archway of sarsaparilla, among vines, indigo plants, beanstalks, creeping lianas, which entwined about our feet like nets. The spongy earth shook around us, and every moment we were nearly swallowed up in quagmires. An infinite number of insects and enormous bats blinded us; rattlesnakes warned from every direction; wolves, bears, wolverines, seeking refuge in these retreats, filled the solitudes with their noises.

Meanwhile it became darker. Low black clouds hung over the darkened woods. The sky was rent with bolts of lightning zigzagging in the heavens. A blustery wind coming from the west rolled cloud upon cloud; the forests bent; the sky opened again and again, and through these rents, we could see new heavens and newer horizons. It was frightening! It was magnificent! A thunderbolt set fire to the woods. The fire spread like hair aflame, columns of fire and smoke spiraled heavenward, and the skies vomited flashes of lightning into the conflagration. Then the Great Spirit covered the mountains with heavy clouds of darkness. From the middle of this chaos rose a confused roar compounded by the howling of the winds, the breaking of the trees, the cries of wild beasts, the crackling of the fire, and the repeated crashes of thunder, which whistled as they hit the waters.

The Great Spirit knows! At this instant I saw only Atala and thought only of her. Under the bent trunk of a birch, I succeeded in protecting her from the torrential rain. Seated under this tree, holding my beloved in my lap, and warming her bare feet with my hands, I was happier than the newlywed who feels for the first time her babe stirring within her womb.

We listened to the noise of the storm; suddenly I felt Atala's tears trickle on my breast. "Tempest of the heart," I cried, "is this a drop of your rain?" Then embracing her whom I loved, "Atala," I said to her, "you hide something from me. Open your heart, my beauteous one! It is so helpful when another can look into our heart! Tell me this secret sorrow about which you are silent. Ah! I know it, you weep for home."

Immediately she replied, "Child of man, how could I weep for my fatherland when my father was not from the land of the palms?"

"What!" I replied with great surprise. "Your father did not come from the land of the palms! Who therefore brought you into the world? Answer!"

Then Atala spoke these words, "Before my mother had offered to Simaghan her marriage gift of thirty mares, twenty buffaloes, one hundred measures of acorn oil, fifty beaver skins, and many other riches, she had known a man of white skin. Moreover, my mother's mother threw water in her face, and compelled her to marry the noble Simaghan, very much like to a king and honored by his people like a spirit. But my mother said to her new husband, 'My womb has conceived; kill me.' Simagham replied, 'May the Great Spirit stay my hand from such a wicked deed. I shall not kill you, I shall cut neither your nose nor your ears. You have been sincere and have not deceived my bed. The fruit of your womb will be mine and I shall visit you only after the bird of the rice fields has flown away, when the thirteenth moon has shown in the heavens!' At this time I came into the world and I began to grow, proud like a Spaniard and an Indian. My mother made me a Christian so that her God and the God of my father would be my God. Then the anguish of love came to look for her, and she descended into the small cave hung with skins from whose bourn no man ever returns."

Such was Atala's story.

"And who was your father, poor orphan?" I asked her. "What was his name among men and among spirits?"

"I have never washed the feet of my father," she answered. "I only know he lived with his sister in Saint Augustine and that he always was faithful to my mother. Philip was his name among the angels and men called him Lopez."

At these words, I cried out and my cries shattered the solitude; the noise of my outburst mingled with the raging of the storm. Pressing Atala to my heart, sobbing, I cried, "O my sister! O daughter of Lopez! Daughter of my benefactor!"

Atala was frightened and asked why I was troubled. But when she discovered that Lopez was this noble host who had adopted me in Saint Augustine and that I left him to be free, she was seized too with confusion and joy.

This fraternal friendship which had come to visit us and to join its love with ours was too much for our hearts. Henceforth Atala's struggles were to become futile: in vain did I feel her lift her hand to her breast and make an unusual gesture; already I had drunk the magic love potion from her lips. With my eyes fixed heavenward, by the light of the thunderbolts, in the presence of the Eternal, I held her in my arms. Nuptial ceremony, worthy of our sorrows and the grandeur of our love: wondrous forests that wave your vines and domes like curtains as a covering for our bed, pines aflame that form torches for our wedding, flooded river, roaring mountains, terrible and sublime nature, were you only a trick concocted to deceive us, and could you hide for an instant in your mysterious horrors the happiness of a man!

Atala gave only feeble resistance; I was feeling for the moment profoundly happy, when suddenly a bolt of lightning followed by a crash of thunder, furrowed the thickness of the shadows and filled the forest with fire and light. It smashed a tree at our feet. We fled.

Then to our surprise in a silence that followed, we heard the ringing of a bell! Bewildered, we both listened to this sound, so strange in the wilderness.

Almost instantly a dog barked in the distance; he was approaching us; his barking became louder, he came up to us, and whined at our feet with joy.

An old hermit, carrying a small lantern, followed him through the darkness of the forest. "May Providence be blessed," he said when he saw us. "I have sought you for a long time! Our dog picked up your scent when the storm began to rage, and he led me here. Good God! How young you are! Poor children! Here, I have brought a bear skin; it will be for the young maiden; here is a little wine in this calabash. May God be praised in all His works! His mercy is indeed great, and His goodness is infinite!"

Atala fell at the feet of the holy man: "Chief of prayer," she said to him, "I am Christian; heaven has sent you to be my salvation."

"My daughter," said the hermit, helping her up, "we ring the mission bells during the night and during storms to call out to strangers; and like our brothers in the Alps and Lebanon Mountains we have taught our dog to look for lost travelers."

As for me, I scarcely understood what the hermit was saying; this love seemed so far beyond the grasp of men that I thought it was all a dream. By the light of a small lantern which the holy man held, I remarked that his beard and hair were all dripping wet; his feet, his hands and face were bloodied from the brambles.

"Old man," I said at last, "how courageous you are. You have no fear of being struck by lightning?"

"Fear!" replied the priest with a kind of warmth. "Fear, when there are men in danger and when I can be of service to them! I would indeed be a most unworthy servant of Jesus Christ!"

"But you know," I said to him, "that I am not Christian!"

"Young man," the hermit replied, "have I inquired of your religious persuasion? Jesus Christ never said, 'My blood will redeem this one, and not that one.' He died for Jew and Gentile, and He saw in all men only brothers and unfortunate creatures. What I do here for you is very little, and you would find better help elsewhere. But the glory for this must not fall upon priests. What are we—weak, lonely ones—if not mean instruments of a celestial work? And what soldier would be cowardly enough to retreat when his leader, cross in hand and brow crowned with thorns, walks before him to help men?"

These words clutched at my heart; tears of admiration and tenderness poured from my eyes.

"My dear children," said the missionary, "in these forests I minister to a small flock of your Indian brothers. My grotto is rather close by in the mountains. Come and warm yourselves at my hearth. You will find none of life's conveniences, but you shall have shelter, and for this we must thank God's divine goodness, for there are many who lack it."

THE TILLERS OF THE SOIL

There are upright men whose conscience is so tranquil that one cannot approach them without sharing in the peace which radiates from their hearts and discourse. As the hermit was speaking, I felt the passions in my breast subside, and even the storm in the heavens seemed to die away with his voice. The clouds were soon scattered enough to allow us to leave our retreat. We left the forest and began to scale the slope of a high mountain. The dog walked ahead of us, carrying the extinguished lantern on the end of a stick. I held Atala's hand, and we followed the missionary. Often he would turn around to look at us, thinking sympathetically of our sorrows and our youth. A book hung about his neck and he leaned on a white walking stick. His posture was erect, his face pale and thin, his appearance simple and sincere. He did not have the lifeless and unobtrusive characteristics of a man born without passions. You could see that his days had been hard, and the wrinkles on his brow were evidence enough of the deep scars of passion healed by virtuous living and by the love of God and man.

When he spoke, standing tall and motionless, his long beard, his eyes humbly lowered, the affectionate tone in his voice, everything about him exuded something calm and sublime. Whoever has seen Father Aubry, as I have, making his way in the wilderness, with his stick and breviary, has a true idea of the Christian vagabond on earth.

After a half-hour of dangerous walking along the mountain paths, we came to the missionary's grotto. We entered through the ivy and gourds, which the rain had disengaged from the rocks. There was nothing here excepting a matting of papaya leaves, a calabash for drawing water, some wooden receptacles, a spade, a domesticated serpent and, on a rock which served as a table, a crucifix and the Book of the Christians.

The man of ancient days hastened to light a fire with some dry vines. He crushed corn with two stones and made a cake, leaving it to cook under the ashes. When the cake was a rich golden color, he served it to us hot, with nut cream in a maple bowl.

Evening brought calm, and the servant of the Great Spirit suggested that we go sit by the entrance to his grotto. We followed him, and from this spot commanded a panoramic view. In the east, the remnants of the storm were scattered in disorder; in the distance, the light of the fire ignited by the lightning still shone; at the foot of the mountain, a wood of pine had been entirely leveled into the silt, and the river swept along pell-mell clods of earth, tree trunks, bodies of animals, and dead fish, whose silvery bellies were floating on the surface of the waters.

It was in this setting that Atala told our story to this old spirit of the mountain. His heart seemed touched, and tears fell upon his beard. "My child," he said to Atala, "you must offer your sufferings to God, in whose honor you have already done so many things. He will accord you repose. See how these forests smoke, how these floods dry, how these clouds are scattering. Do you think that He who can calm such a storm will not be able to calm the troubled heart of man? If you have no better retreat, my dear daughter, I offer you a place among the flock which I have had the good fortune to call to Jesus Christ. I shall instruct Chactas and I shall give him to you for a husband when he is worthy of you."

At these words, I fell at the feet of the hermit, weeping tears of joy. But Atala became pale as death. Kindly the old hermit raised me, and then I noticed that his hands were mutilated. Atala understood at once his sorrows. "Barbarians!" she cried.

"My daughter," replied the priest with a warm smile, "what is this compared with the sufferings of my Divine Master? If heathen Indians have tortured me, they are poor blind creatures whom God one day will enlighten. The more they have made me suffer, the more proportionately I love them. I could not remain in my own country, to which I returned, and where its illustrious queen did me the honor of wanting to see these insignificant signs of my apostolate. And what more glorious reward could I receive for my work than permission from the head of our religion to celebrate the divine sacrifice with these mutilated hands? After such an honor there remains nothing but to try to make myself worthy of the privilege. I have come back to the New World to use the rest of my life in the service of my God. I have lived in this solitude for nearly thirty years, and to-morrow it will be twenty-two years since I made this rock my home. When I arrived here, I found only wandering families whose customs were savage, whose way of life was extremely miserable. I have taught them the meaning of peace, and their customs have gradually been mollified. They live now grouped together at the foot of this mountain. While instructing them in the ways of salvation, I have tried to teach them the rudimentary arts of living, but without taking them too far, and still preserving in these good people that simplicity which brings happiness. As for me, afraid of annoying them by my presence, I have kept to this grotto, where they come for my advice. It is here, far from men, that I worship God in the grandeur of these solitudes, and prepare for the death which my old age announces."

When he finished speaking, the hermit knelt, and we did so, too. He began to recite a prayer, to which Atala made responses. Silent flashes of lightning still opened the heavens in the east, and over the western clouds three suns shone together. Some foxes scattered by the storm stretched their black noses over the edge of the precipice. You could hear the rustling of plants, which, drying in the evening breeze, lifted their fallen stems.

We went back into the grotto, where the hermit made a bed of cypress moss for Atala. A profound languor emanated from the eyes and movements of this maiden. She looked at Father Aubry as if she wanted to divulge a secret. But something seemed to restrain her, either my presence, or a certain shame, or the futility of the confession. I heard her get up in the middle of the night; she went looking for the hermit, but as he had given her his bed, he had gone to the mountain to contemplate the beauty of the heavens and to pray. He told me the following day that it was his custom, even in wintertime, to do so, since he loved to watch the forests waving their naked treetops, the clouds racing across the heavens, and to hear the winds and the streams murmuring in

the solitude. My sister was obliged to go back to her
bed where she slumbered. Alas! Filled with hope,
I saw in Atala's weakness only the passing signs of
weariness!

The following morning I arose to the singing of the
cardinals and hummingbirds nesting in the acacias
and laurel trees that grew all around the grotto. I went
to pick a magnolia and placed it, wet with the tears
of the morning, on the head of the still sleeping Atala.
I hoped, according to the religion of my country, that
the soul of some child who had died at the breast
would descend upon this flower in a dewdrop and
that a happy dream might carry it into the bosom of
my future wife. I then went looking for our host. I
found him with his robe gathered into his two pockets,
his rosary beads in hand; seated on the trunk of a pine
tree which had fallen because of age, he was waiting
for me. He suggested that I go with him to the mission
while Atala was still asleep. I accepted, and we started
at once.

Going down the mountain, I noticed some oaks on
which the spirits seemed to have carved some strange
figures. The hermit told me that he had carved them
himself, and that they were some verses of the ancient
poet, Homer, and some sayings from a still more
ancient poet, Solomon. There was a certain mysterious harmony between this wisdom of the ages,
these verses covered by moss, this old hermit who had
carved them, and these old oak trees which served
him as books.

His name, his age, and the date of his mission were
also marked on a reed of the savannah at the foot of
these trees. I was astonished at the fragility of this
last monument: "It will last," he replied to me, "longer than I, and it will always be of more worth than
the little good on earth I have accomplished."

From here we proceeded to the entrance of a valley, where I saw a wonderful sight. It was a natural bridge, like the one in Virginia, of which you have perhaps heard. Men, my son, especially those in your country, often imitate nature, and reproductions are always trivial. It is not so with nature, when she seems to be imitating the works of men, she is actually offering models. It is then that she throws a bridge from the top of one mountain to the top of another, suspends roads in the clouds, spreads rivers for canals, sculptures mountains for columns, and for pools, digs out seas.

We passed under the arch of this bridge and found ourselves before another marvel. It was the cemetery for the Indians of the mission or the *Groves of Death*. Father Aubry had permitted his neophytes to bury their dead in their accustomed manner and to preserve for the place of burial its Indian name. Only he had sanctified this spot with a cross. The ground was divided, like the community fields of harvests, into as many plots as there were families. Each plot was in itself a wooded area which varied according to the taste of those who planted it. A stream meandered quietly around these groves; they called it the *Stream of Peace*. This charming haven for the dead was bounded on the east by the bridge under which we had passed; two hills enclosed it to the north and south; it opened only to the west where a large forest of pine trees rose majestically. The trunks of these trees, red and veined with green, rising without branches to their tops, resembled high columns and formed the peristyle of this temple of death. Like the muffled sounds of the organ underneath the vaults of a church, a religious tonality reigned here. But, as you penetrated into the depths of this sanctuary, only the hymns of the birds honoring the memory

of the departed could be heard in an eternal cele-
bration.

As we left this forest, we came upon the mission
village, located on the banks of a lake, in the midst
of a savannah bright with flowers. We arrived there
through an avenue of magnolias and live oaks which
bordered one of the ancient roads found near the
mountains dividing Kentucky from the Floridas. As
soon as the Indians caught sight of their shepherd
in the plain, they abandoned their work and ran to
meet him. Some kissed his robe, others helped him
walk; mothers lifted their little ones in their arms to
let them see this man of Jesus Christ who was shedding
tears. As he walked along with them, he inquired
about what was going on in the village; he gave advice
to this one, gently reprimanded another; he spoke of
the harvesting, of teaching the children, of consoling
the suffering. In all his conversation he spoke of God.

Thus escorted, we reached the foot of a huge cross
which was by the road. It was here that the servant of
God was accustomed to celebrate the mysteries of his
religion. "My beloved neophytes," he said, turning
toward the gathering, "there come to you a brother
and a sister, and to crown your good fortune, I see
that Providence yesterday spared your harvests. Here
are two good reasons for giving thanks to Him. Let
us, therefore, offer up the holy sacrifice, and let each
bring to this sacrifice a profound meditation, a living
faith, infinite thanks, and a humble heart."

Immediately the holy priest put on a white tunic
of mulberry bark; the sacred vessels were taken from
a tabernacle at the foot of the cross; the altar was
prepared on a section of a rock; water was drawn
from the nearby stream; and a bunch of wild grapes
furnished the wine for the sacrifice. We knelt down
in the tall grass. The holy rites began.

Dawn, appearing behind the mountains, set the east afire. Everything was gold or softly pink in the solitude. The morning sun, announced by so much splendor, finally made its appearance from behind a vastness of light, and its first ray touched the consecrated host, which the priest at that moment was was lifting heavenward. O charm of religion! O magnificence of Christian worship! For a celebrant, an old hermit; for an altar, a rock; for a church, the wilderness; for a congregation, innocent savages! No, I cannot doubt that, when we prostrated ourselves, the great mystery was fulfilled and that God did come down to us on earth. I felt Him come into my heart.

After the sacrifice, at which I missed only the daughter of Lopez, we returned to the village. There reigned the most touching blending of social and natural life. In the corner of a cypress grove in an ancient wilderness, one noticed a new growth. Ears of grain swayed in golden waves over the trunk of a fallen oak; thus the sheaf of a summer replaced the tree of three centuries. Everywhere one could see the forests delivered to flames, sending up heavy banks of smoke, and the plow going its way slowly among the remains of the roots. Surveyors with long chains went to measure the land. Arbitrators were setting up the first properties. The bird gave up its nest, and the lair of the wild beast was changed to a cabin. Forges were rumbling. Blows of the ax, for the last time, made reverberate echoes which died away like the trees.

I wandered with delight amid these scenes, made all the sweeter by thoughts of Atala and dreams of bliss which lulled my heart. I stood in awe of the triumph of Christianity over primitive life. I saw the Indian becoming civilized through the voice of religion. I was attending the primal marriage feast of man and earth: man, by this sacred contract, yielding to the earth the fruit of his sweating; the earth, in return, agreeing to bear faithfully man's harvests, his sons and his ashes.

Meanwhile, they presented an infant to the missionary, who baptized it among the blooming jasmine by the edge of a brook; meanwhile, in the midst of the games and work, a coffin moved to the *Groves of Death*. A couple received the nuptial blessing beneath an oak, and then we went to settle them in a corner of the wilderness. The pastor walked ahead of us, blessing here and there the rock, the tree, and the fountain, just as a long time ago, according to the Book of the Christians, God blessed the uncultivated earth when He gave it to Adam for his heritage. These people with their flocks, making a disorderly procession as they followed their venerable leader from rock to rock, touched me and brought to mind the migration of the first families, when Shem was making his way with his children through an unknown world, following the sun which led him.

I wanted to know from this holy hermit how he governed his children. He answered me with kindness: "I have given them no law. I have taught them only to love one another, to pray to God, and to hope for a better life. All the laws of the world are contained in these precepts. You see in the middle of the village a cabin larger than the others: it serves as a chapel in the rainy season. We gather there morning and night to praise the Lord. When I am not there an old man leads them in prayer, for age, like maternity, is a kind of priesthood. Then we go work in our fields, and although properties are divided, in order that each one may learn social economy, harvests are put in common granaries to promote brotherly love. Four elders distribute equitably the fruits of labor. Add to this religious ceremonies, many hymns, the cross where I celebrate the mysteries, the elm tree under which I preach when the weather is good, our graves close by our wheat fields, our rivers in which I dip the little children and the Saint Johns of this new Bethany—you will have a complete idea of this kingdom of Jesus Christ.

The words of the hermit delighted me, and I knew at once the superiority of this stable, busy life over the wandering, idle life of the savage.

Ah, René, I do not murmur against Providence; but I confess that I never recall that evangelical society without experiencing some pangs of regret. How happy my life would have been with Atala along those shores! There I should have finished all my wanderings! There, with my beloved, unknown to men, hiding my happiness in the depth of the forests, I would have passed my years as these nameless rivers flow in the wilds. Instead of this tranquility which I dared to promise myself, into what troubles my days were plunged! A constant toy of chance, I was dashed against every river bank, exiled for a long time from my country, only to find there, on my return, merely a cabin in ruins and friends in the grave—such was to be the destiny of Chactas.

THE DRAMA

If my dream of happiness was bright, it was also short-lived, and a rude awakening awaited me at the hermit's grotto. When we arrived in the middle of the day, I was surprised not to see Atala come running to greet us. A certain sudden terror seized me. Approaching the grotto, I dared not call out to Atala: my imagination was likewise gripped with terror at the sound or the silence that would attend my cries. Frightened still more by the darkness in the entrance of the cave, I said to the missionary: "O you whom Heaven accompanies and strengthens, enter these shadows."

How weak he is whom passions rule! How strong he is who rests in the Lord! There was more courage in that religious heart, withered by its seventy-six years, than in all the ardor of my youth. The man of peace entered the grotto, and I remained outside full of terror. Soon a feeble murmur, like moans, came from the depths of the grotto, and struck my ears.

Giving out a cry and finding strength, I hurried into the darkness of the cave. . . . Spirits of my fathers, you alone know the sight that struck my eyes!

The hermit had lit a pine torch, he held it in his trembling hand, above Atala's couch. This beautiful young maiden, half raised on her elbow, was pale and disheveled. Beads of feverish sweat gleamed on her forehead. Her lusterless eyes tried yet to express her love for me, and her mouth tried to smile. Stunned as though struck by a thunderbolt, blankly staring, my arms outstretched, and my lips parted, I stood immobile. For a moment a profound silence was held by these three characters of this sorrowful scene. The hermit was the first to break it: "This is probably only a fever brought about from fatigue, and if we resign ourselves to the will of God, he will have pity upon us."

At these words, the blood stopped in my veins began to flow again, and with the mobility of a savage, I passed from a state of extreme fear to one of extreme confidence. But Atala did not for long leave me confident. Sadly shaking her head, she made a sign that we should approach her couch.

"My father," she said weakly to the holy priest, "I'm about to die. O Chactas, hear without despairing the terrible secret which I have kept from you. I have kept my secret so as not to hurt you and to obey my mother. Try not to interrupt me with signs of your sorrow. They would only shorten the few moments I have to live. I have many things to tell, and by these heart beats which grow weaker—by some icy weight which my breast can hardly lift—I feel that I must hurry."

After some moments of silence, Atala continued: "My sad fate began almost before I saw the light of day. My mother conceived me in sorrow; I wearied her womb, and she brought me into the world with great rendings of her body. They despaired of my life. To save me, my mother made a vow: she promised the Queen of the Angels that I should consecrate to her my virginity, if I should be spared from death . . . a fatal vow which hastens me to my grave!

"I began my sixteenth year when I lost my mother. Some hours before her death, she called me to her bedside. 'My daughter,' she said to me in the presence of a missionary who was administering to her last minutes, 'you know about the vow I made for you. Would you have your mother dishonored? O my Atala, I leave you behind in a world unworthy of a Christian girl, in the midst of heathens who persecute the God of your fathers and mine, the God who, having given you life, has preserved you by a miracle. Ah, my dear child, when you accept the veil of virgins, you give up only the cares of the cabin and the terrible passions which have troubled your mother's womb! Come, my beloved daughter, come and swear by the image of the Saviour's mother, between the hands of this holy priest and your dying mother, that you will not betray me in the face of Heaven. Remember that I promised for you in order to save your life, and that if you do not keep my promise, you shall plunge the soul of your mother into everlasting torments.'

"O my mother, why did you speak to me thus! O religion which at once is my sorrow and happiness, which destroys and comforts me! And you, fond and sad object of a passion which consumes me even to the arms of death, you see now, O Chactas, what has made our fate so implacable! . . .

"Bursting into tears and throwing myself on my mother's breast, I promised everything she wished. The missionary pronounced over me the fearful words and he gave me the scapular which bound me forever. My mother threatened me with her curse if ever I should break my vow. And then enjoining me to keep my secret inviolate from the heathens, persecutors of my religion, she died, holding me in her arms.

"I did not realize the danger of my oaths. Full of fervor, and Christian by conviction, proud of the Spanish blood which coursed through my veins, I only saw about me men unworthy of my hand. I rejoiced in having no other husband but the God of my mother. I saw you, young and handsome prisoner; I grieved for your fate; I dared speak to you by the stake in the forest; then did I feel the weight of my oaths."

When Atala finished speaking, clenching my fists and fixing my eyes on the missionary threateningly, I cried at him: "So this is the religion of which you have boasted to me! Perish the oath which takes Atala from me! Perish the God who thwarts nature! Man, priest, why did you come into these forests?"

"To save you," said the old man in a terrible voice, "to subdue your passions, to prevent you, blasphemer, from bringing upon yourself the wrath of God! It becomes you, young man, hardly grown up, to complain of your misfortunes! Where are the marks of your sufferings? Where are the injustices you have suffered? Where are your virtues, which alone could give you some right to complain? What services have you rendered? What good have you done? Eh? Wretched one, you offer me only your passions, and you dare storm the gates of Heaven! When, like Father Aubry, you have spent thirty years exiled in the mountains, you will be less prompt to pass judgment on the purposes of divine Providence. Then you will understand that you know nothing, that you are nothing, and that there is no punishment so severe, no misfortunes so terrible, which our corrupt flesh does not deserve to suffer."

Flashes of light bolted from the eyes of the old priest; his beard beat against his chest; his terrifying words made him like a god. Overwhelmed by his majesty, I fell at his feet and asked him to pardon my violent outbursts. "My son," he replied in such a gentle tone that remorse gripped my heart, "it is not for myself that I have reprimanded you. Alas, you are right, my dear child: I have done little good in these forests, and God has no servant more unworthy than I. But, my son, it is against Heaven, against Heaven that you must never rebel! Pardon me if I have offended you, but let us listen to your sister. There is perhaps some escape; let us never tire of hoping. Chactas, it is a divine religion which has made a virtue of hope!"

"My young friend," continued Atala, "you have been witness to my struggles and moreover you have seen the smallest part of them. I have hidden the rest from you. No, the black slave who waters with his sweat the burning sands of Florida is less miserable than was your Atala. I encouraged you to escape, knowing full well I should die if you left me. I feared to flee with you into the wilderness, and yet I yearned for the shade of its woods. . . . Ah! If I had only to quit my parents, friends, and country, if even—a horrible thought—there had been only the loss of my soul! But your shadow, O my mother, your shadow hovered over me, always reproaching me with its torments! I listened to your cries, I saw the fires of hell enveloping you. My nights were arid and full of phantoms; my days were desolate; the dew of the evening dried when it touched upon my burning skin. I parted my lips to the breezes, and the breezes, far from giving them freshness, caught fire from my breath. What torment seeing you, Chactas, constantly by my side, far from all men, in the depths of these solitudes, and feeling between you and me an invincible barrier! To spend my life at your feet, to serve you as your slave, to prepare your meals and your couch in some forgotten corner of the universe, would have been my supreme happiness. This happiness was all mine, but I could not enjoy it. What plans did I not make! What dreams did not arise from the recesses of my sad heart! Sometimes, fixing my eyes upon you, I even went so far as to formulate desires as wild as they were blameworthy: sometimes I would have wished to be the only living creature on earth with you; sometimes, sensing a divinity was arresting my horrible transports, I would have wished that this divinity be annihilated, providing, however, that locked in your arms, I could have plunged from one abyss to another with God's debris and the world's. Even now . . . shall I confess it? Even now when eternity is about to swallow me, when I am about to appear before my inexorable Judge, at this moment when, to obey my mother, I see joyfully my virginity consuming my life; ah well! by some frightful contradiction, I sweep aside the regret for not having been yours!"

"My daughter," interrupted the missionary, "your sorrow misguides you. This extreme passion to which you have abandoned yourself is seldom correct; it is not even natural, and therefore it is less blameworthy in the eyes of God, because it is rather an error of reasoning than a vice of the heart. You must rid yourself of these angry transports which are unworthy of your innocence. But also, my dear child, your impetuous imagination has alarmed you too much concerning your vows. Religion does not demand superhuman sacrifices. Its true feelings, its temperate virtues, far transcend the fanatic feelings and insincere virtues, of false heroism. Supposing you had succumbed, poor lost lamb, the Good Shepherd would have sought you to bring you back to the fold. The treasures of repentence were open to you. Torrents of blood are needed to wash away our faults in the eyes of men; one tear alone is enough for God. Courage, therefore, my dear daughter, your plight requires calmness. Let us speak to God, who cures all the wounds of His servants. If it is His will, as I hope it is, that you recover from this illness, I shall write to the Bishop of Quebec. He has the necessary powers to relieve you from your vows—which are only simple vows—and you shall finish out your days beside me with Chactas for your husband."

When the old man had finished, Atala was seized by a long convulsion from which she came out only to give indications of terrible suffering. "What," she said, joining her hands passionately, "there is a remedy? I could be released from my vows?"

"Yes, my child," said the priest, "and you can still."

"It is too late, too late," she cried. "Must I die when I am learning that I should have been able to be happy? Oh, had I known this saintly man sooner! Today, what happiness I would be enjoying with you, with Chactas a Christian . . . consoled, reassured by this venerable priest . . . in this wilderness . . . for always. . . . Oh! It would have been too much bliss."

"Be calm," I said to her, taking one of her hands. "Be calm, this happiness we shall have together."

"Never, never!" said Atala.

"What?" I stopped her.

"You do not know the whole of it," she cried. "Yesterday . . . during the storm . . . I wanted to break my vows, I wanted to plunge my mother into the depths of the flames; already her curse was upon me, already I lied to God who saved my life ... When you kissed my trembling lips, you did not know, you could not know, that you were embracing death!"

"O Heaven," cried the missionary, "dear child, what have you done?"

"I have committed a crime, Father," said Atala with eyes distraught; "but I was destroying only myself and saving my mother."

"Go on," I cried full of fear.

"Well," she said, "I foresaw my weakness, and when I left the cabins, I took with me ..."

"What?" I said with horror.

"Poison?" asked the priest.

"It is in my breast," cried Atala.

The torch dropped from the hermit's hand. I fell beside the daughter of Lopez. The old man took us both in his arms, and together, in the shadows over this funeral bed, we mingled our sobs.

"Let us awaken, let us awaken," said the courageous hermit, lighting a lamp. "We are losing precious moments: fearless Christians, let us brave the assaults of adversity; with cords about our necks, ashes on our brows, let us throw ourselves at the feet of the Most High, to implore His mercy or to submit ourselves to His decrees. Perhaps there is still time. My daughter, you should have told us last evening."

"Alas, Father," said Atala, "I looked for you last night, but Heaven, to punish my crimes, took you away from me. Besides, all help would have been futile; for the Indians themselves, so skillful in matters of poison, do not know of any remedy for the poison I have taken. O Chactas, imagine my astonishment when I saw that the blow did not come as suddenly as I had expected. My love increased my strength, my soul could not so quickly part from you."

No longer did I interrupt Atala's tale with my sobs, but with outcryings known only to Indians. I rolled with fury on the ground, twisting my arms and biting my hands. The old priest, with a marvelous tenderness, ran from brother to sister, and heaped upon us a thousand cares. In the calm of his heart and under the weight of years, he knew how to speak to our youth, and his religion furnished him with accents more tender and fervent than our own passions. Does not this priest, who for forty years immolated himself each day in the service of God and men of these mountains, recall to you those holocausts of Israel, smoking perpetually in high places before the Lord?

Alas! It was in vain that he tried to bring some remedy to Atala's ills. Fatigue, sorrow, poison, and a passion more deadly than all the poisons together conspired to pluck this flower from our solitude. Toward evening, frightening symptons were in evidence; a general numbness spread through Atala's limbs, and the extremities of her body began to grow cold.

"Touch my fingers," she said to me. "Are they not quite cold?" I did not know what to answer. My hair bristled with horror. Then she added: "Yesterday, my beloved, your touch made me quiver, and now I can no longer feel your hand; I can hardly hear your voice; objects in the grotto are disappearing one by one. Are those not birds singing? Is not the sun about to set? Chactas, its rays, how beautiful they will be, falling lonely on my grave!"

Atala, noticing how these words brought tears to our eyes, said: "You must excuse me, my good friends. I am weak indeed, but perhaps I shall grow stronger. Yet to die so young, when my heart was so full of life! Leader of prayer, have pity on me; remember me. Do you think my mother will be happy, and that God will pardon my offenses?"

"My daughter," replied the good priest, his eyes filled with tears, which he brushed away with trembling, mutilated fingers, "my daughter, all your sorrows come from ignorance. It was your primitive education and the lack of necessary instruction which has destroyed you. You did not know that a Christian cannot dispose of his life as he wishes. Therefore, be consoled, my lamb; God will forgive you because of your sincerity. Your mother and the misguided missionary who advised you were more guilty than you; they went beyond their rights when they extracted from you this senseless vow. But may the peace of the Lord be with them! You offer, all three of you, a terrible example of the dangers of excess and the want of light in matters of religion. Be comforted, my child; He who probes the loins and the heart will judge your intentions, which were pure, but not your action, which was reprehensible.

"As for your life, if the moment has come for you to sleep in the Lord, ah, my dear child, you lose little in losing this world! In spite of the solitude in which you have lived, you have known sorrows. What would you have thought, if you had been a witness to the evils of society, if on arrival on the shores of Europe your ear had heard the long cry of suffering rising out of that old land? Whether he lives in a cave or a palace, everyone suffers, everyone bewails his lot. Queens have been seen to weep like simple women, and you would be astonished at the quantity of tears stored in the eyes of kings!

"Is it your love you regret? My daughter, you might as well cry over a dream. Do you know the heart of a man, and could you number the changes of his desires? You could more easily count the number of waves rolled by the sea in a storm. Atala, our sacrifices and our blessings are not eternal bonds. One day, perhaps, disgust would have followed in the wake of satiety, the past would have counted for nothing, and you would have felt only the inconveniences of a meager and despised union. There is no doubt, my daughter, but that the most beautiful love was that of a man and a woman formed by the hand of the Creator. A paradise had been fashioned for them, they were innocent and immortal. Perfect in soul and body, they were suited for each other in every way. Eve had been created for Adam, and Adam for Eve. If they were unable to continue in that state of happiness, what couple after that could? I will not speak to you of the marriages of the first-born of men, of those unutterable unions, when the sister was the wife of the brother, when fraternal love and friendship were confounded in the same heart, and when the purity of the one increased the delights of the other. All these unions were fraught with sorrows. Jealousy crept to the grass altar on which the kid was sacrificed; she ruled under the tent of Abraham and even over the beds where patriachs enjoyed such pleasures that they were unmindful of the death of their mothers.

"Would you delude yourself, my child, in being more innocent and happier in your ties than those holy families from which Jesus Christ chose to descend. I spare you the details of the household cares, the quarrels, the mutual reproaches, the anxieties, and all those hidden sorrows which hover over the pillow of the nuptial bed. Woman renews her sorrow each time she becomes a mother. She marries in tears. What grief is the loss of a newborn to whom you have given your milk and who dies at your breast! The mountain was filled with lamentations, nothing could console Rachel because her sons lived no more. These bitternesses accompanying all our human affections are so strong that I have seen in my country great ladies loved by kings leave the Court to bury themselves in cloisters and to chastise their rebellious flesh, whose pleasures led only to sorrows.

"But perhaps you will say that these last examples do not touch you, that your ambition was only to live in an obscure cabin with the man of your choice, that you were seeking less the sweet pleasures of marriage than the charms of this madness which youth calls love. Illusion, fancy, vanity, dream of a wounded imagination! I, too, my daughter, I have known the sorrows of the heart: this head was not always bald, nor this breast as calm as it seems today. Trust in my experience. If man, constant in his affections, could ceaselessly bring to his feelings a newness, undoubtedly solitude and love would equal him to God, for these are the two eternal pleasures of the Supreme Being. But the soul of man wearies, and never for a long time does it love the same object fully. There are always points where two hearts never meet, and these points suffice to make life unbearable.

"Finally, my dear child, the great mistake of men, in their quest for happiness, is to forget the infirmity of their nature: you must die. Sooner or later, whatever has been your happiness, this beautiful countenance would have changed to that uniform face which the sepulcher gives to the family of Adam. Even the eye of Chactas would not have been able to recognize you among your sisters of the grave. Love has no dominion over the worms in the coffin. What am I saying—O vanities of vanities! Why have I spoken of the power of earthly friendships? Do you wish, my daughter, to know the extent of them? If a man came back to life several years after his death, I doubt if he would be welcomed with joy by the very persons who had shed the most tears in his memory. As quickly as we form other ties, so we easily take on other habits; just as inconstancy is natural to man, so our life is a small thing even in the hearts of our friends!

"Therefore, my dear daughter, thank Divine Goodness for taking you so early from this vale of tears. Already the white robe and gleaming crown of virgins are being prepared for you in the clouds; already I hear the Queen of Angels, whose voice is calling you: 'Come, my worthy servant, come, my dove, come and sit ye down on the throne of candor, among all those fair maidens who have sacrificed their beauty and youth to the service of humanity, to the education of children and to the great works of penitence. Come, mystical rose, rest your head on the bosom of Christ. This coffin, a nuptial bed which you have chosen, will never be dishonored, and the embraces of your heavenly husband will be without end!' "

As the last rays of the day soften the winds and spread their peaceful mantle around the vault of heaven, so the quiet speech of the old priest subdued the passions in the breast of my loved one. She seemed now only occupied with my sadness and with means to help me sustain her loss. Sometimes she whispered she would die happily if I promised her to dry my tears; sometimes she spoke to me of her mother, of my country; she sought to distract me from my woes by awakening in me a sorrow of the past. She exhorted me to patience, to virtue. "You will not always be wretched," she said. "If Heaven tries you today, it is only to make you more compassionate for the sorrows of others. The heart, O Chactas, is like those trees which give their balm for the wounds of men only when the iron has wounded them!"

When she had so spoken, she turned toward the missionary, looking for the comfort she had just rendered to me, and being consoled and consoling, she gave and received the word of life on her deathbed.

Meanwhile the hermit redoubled his zeal. His ancient bones were enlivened by the ardor of charity, and as he prepared remedies, relit the fire, and freshened her bed, he spoke fervently of God and the righteousness of His ways. With the torch of his faith in hand, he seemed to be guiding Atala to her grave to show her its beauteous secrets. The humble grotto was filled with the light of this Christian death, and the heavenly spirits were of course looking down upon this scene where religion struggled alone with love, youth, and death.

Thus divine religion triumphed, and we were conscious of its victory, as a holy sadness possessed our hearts after the first transports of passion. Toward the middle of the night, Atala seemed to revive. She repeated the prayers which the priest pronounced by her bedside. A little while afterward, she held my hand, and in a voice scarcely audible, she said, "Son of Outalissi, do you recall that first night when you took me for the Maiden of Last Love? What a strange omen of our destiny!" She stopped, then went on, "When I reflect that I am leaving you for always, my heart makes such an effort to go on living that I almost feel the power of becoming immortal by the sheer force of my love. But, my God, may Your will be done!" Atala, silent for a few moments, added, "I have no more to ask of you but forgiveness for the woes I have brought upon you. By my pride and caprices I have tormented you too much. Chactas, a little earth over my body will put a world between us and free you from the burden of my misfortunes."

"To forgive you!" I said to her with tears streaming down my cheeks. "Is it not I who have caused you all these torments?"

"My friend," she interrupted, "you have made me supremely happy, and had I my life to live again, I would choose again to love you for a few brief moments in exile rather than to live a life of contentment in my native land."

Here Atala's voice died away. The shadows of death lurked about her eyes and mouth. Her groping fingers reached for something to touch. She talked in whispers to invisible spirits. Soon, with much effort, she tried in vain to detach the small crucifix from her neck. She begged me to untie it and then said, "When I spoke to you the first time, you saw on my breast this cross shining in the light of the fire. It is my only worldly possession. Lopez, your father and mine, sent it to my mother a few days after my birth. Receive this inheritance, my brother; keep it in memory of my sorrows. You shall have recourse to this God of the unfortunate in the trials of your life. Chactas, I have one last request to make of you. Friend, our union would have been short on earth, but there is after this life a longer one. How terrible it would be to be separated from you forever! Today I am only going before you, and I shall await you in the celestial kingdom. If you have loved me, be instructed in the Christian religion, which shall prepare our reunion. Before your very eyes this religion works miracles, since it renders me capable of quitting you without dying in the terrible anguish of despair. Yet, Chactas, I would require of you only a simple promise, for I know only too well the price of an oath. Perhaps a vow would separate you from some woman more fortunate than I. . . . O my mother, pardon your daughter. O Virgin of Heaven, hold back your anger. I am falling into my old weakness and I am robbing Thee, O my God, of thoughts which should be Thine alone!"

Broken with grief, I promised Atala that I would one day embrace the Christian religion.

Watching, the hermit arose solemnly, and lifting his arms to the vault of the grotto, said, "It is time, it is time to call God here!"

Scarcely had he pronounced these words when a supernatural power constrained me to fall to my knees, and I bowed my head at the foot of Atala's couch. The priest opened a hidden box containing a golden receptacle, covered with a silken veil. He prostrated himself and worshiped fervently. Suddenly the grotto seemed aglow. Voices of the angels and celestial strains of the harp were heard in the air. When the hermit took the sacred vessel from his tabernacle, I thought I saw God himself coming from the side of the mountain.

The priest opened the ciborium. He took between his two fingers a host white as snow and went over to Atala, pronouncing strange words. She raised her eyes ecstatically to heaven. All her sorrows seemed suspended. All her life seemed centered in the expression on her face, and reverently she reached for her God, hidden in the mystical bread. Then the holy priest dipped a small piece of cotton into the consecrated oil and anointed her temples. For a moment he watched the dying girl, and suddenly uttered these awesome words: "Depart, Christian soul, go and join your Creator!"

Raising my head and looking at the vessel containing the holy oil, I cried out, "Father, will this remedy bring her back to life?"

"Yes, my son," said the old man, falling into my arms, "to life everlasting."

Atala was dead.

At this point, for the second time since the beginning of the narrative, Chactas was obliged to interrupt. His tears flowed, and his voice gave forth half-articulated words. The blind sachem opened his mantle and drew out Atala's crucifix.

Here it is, he said, this token of adversity! O René, my son, you see it; and I, I see it no more! Tell me, after so many years, has not the gold changed? Can you not see upon it the marks of my teardrops? Can you recognize the spot where her saintly lips touched it? And why is Chactas not yet a Christian? What trivial reasons of politics and patriotism have kept me till now in the errors of my fathers? Now, I will not delay any longer. The earth cries out to me, "When will you descend to the grave and why do you still wait to embrace a divine religion?" O earth, you shall not wait for long. As soon as a priest has made young again with waters this head white with sorrows, I shall join Atala. But let us finish what remains to be told of my story.

THE FUNERAL

I shall not attempt, O René, to paint for you today the despair which possessed my soul when Atala gave up her last sigh. I would need more fervor than I have, my closed eyes would have to open again to the sun to ask of it an account of the tears they shed in its light. Yes, this moon shining now overhead will grow weary of lighting up the solitudes of Kentucky; yes, this river now bearing our canoes will stop the flow of its waters before my tears stop their flow for Atala! For two whole days, I was insensible to the hermit's conversation. Trying to assuage my sorrows, this excellent man never descended to the vain reasonings of this world; he only said, "My son, it is God's will," and he held me in his arms. I should never have believed there was so much consolation in these few words of a resigned Christian, had I not experienced it myself.

The tenderness, the consolation, the unfaltering patience of the old servant of God at last conquered the obstinacy of my sorrow. I was ashamed of the tears I caused him to shed for me. "Father," I said, "I have gone too far. May the passions of a young man never more trouble the peace of your days. Let me bear away the remains of my loved one. I shall bury them in some corner of the wilderness, and should I still be condemned to live, I shall try to make myself worthy of the eternal wedding promised to me by Atala."

At this unhoped-for return of courage, the good father leaped for joy. "O Blood of Christ!" he cried. "Blood of my divine Master, I recognize in this Thy goodness! You will save this man, my God, fulfill Thy work; I give peace to his troubled soul, and leave him only humble and useful memories of his grief!"

The good man refused me the body of Lopez's daughter, but he suggested that we summon his neophytes and bury her with all Christian solemnity. I refused in my turn. "Atala's sorrows and virtues," I said to him, "were unknown to men; let her grave, dug by our hands secretly, partake of this same obscurity!" We agreed to go the following morning at sunrise to bury our Atala under the arch of the natural bridge, at the entrance to the *Groves of Death*. It was also decided that we should spend the night in prayer by the body of this holy one.

Toward evening, we carried her precious remains to the opening of the grotto which faced to the north. The hermit had wrapped them in a piece of European linen, woven by his mother; it was the only possession he had from his native land, and for a long time he had intended it for his own burial. Atala was laid on a carpet of mountain mimosa. Her feet, her head, her shoulders, and a part of her breast were uncovered. In her hair she wore a wilted magnolia flower . . . the very one I had placed on the bed of this maiden to render her fertile. Her lips, like pink buds picked two mornings ago, seemed to languish and smile. On her cheeks so white some blue veins showed. Her beautiful eyes were closed, her modest feet joined together, and her alabaster hands pressed to her heart a crucifix of ebony. The scapular of her vows was passed about her neck. She seemed enchanted by the Angel of Melancholy and by the twin sleep of innocence and the grave. I have never seen anything more celestial. Whoever had not known that this young maiden had once enjoyed the light of day would have taken her for a sleeping statue of virginity.

The holy man never ceased his prayers the whole night. I was seated in reverent silence at the head of my Atala's funeral bed. How many times, while she slept, had I held in my lap her lovely head! How many times had I bent over her to hear and to inhale her breath! But now no sound came from her motionless breast, and in vain did I wait for this beauty to awake!

The pale moon was a torch to our funeral watch. It rose in the middle of the night like a white vestal come to weep at the coffin of her companion. Soon it spread through the woods its great secret of melancholy, which it loves to tell to the old oaks and ancient shores of the sea. From time to time, the holy man dipped a flowered twig into consecrated water, and shaking the wet branch, perfumed the night with heavenly balms. Sometimes he would repeat in ancient rhythms some verses of the old poet Job:

"I have passed away like a flower, I have withered like the grass in the fields.
"Why has light been given to the miserable and life to those whose souls are filled with bitterness?"

Thus sang the ancient of men. His solemn chanting voice intoned through the silence of the wilderness. The name of God uttered at this tomb echoed back from all the waters and from all the forests. The cooings of the Virginia dove, the cascading of the waterfalls on the mountain, the tolling of the bell to summon travelers, blended with these funereal chants. And in the *Groves of Death* one could almost hear the distant choir of the departed answering the voice of the hermit.

Meanwhile a golden bar formed in the east. Sparrow hawks called from their rocks and martins returned to their nests in the elms; it was the signal for Atala's funeral cortège. I lifted her body to my shoulders; the hermit walked before me, a spade in his hand. We began our descent from rock to rock. Old age and death slackened our pace. At the sight of the dog who had found us in the forest, and who now, jumping joyously, was leading us by another way, I burst into tears. Often Atala's long hair, plaything of the morning breezes, spread its golden veil before my eyes; often, bending beneath the weight, I was constrained to set it down on the moss and to sit beside it to recover my strength. Finally, we arrived at the spot marked by my sorrow; we descended under the arch of the bridge. O my son! Imagine a young Indian and an old hermit, on their knees, opposite each other, digging with their hands a grave for a poor maiden whose body was outstretched nearby, in a ravine dried of its waters!

When our task was accomplished, we carried beautiful Atala to her earthy bed. Alas! I had hoped to prepare another couch for her! Taking a little dirt in my hand, and with terrible silence, for the last time I gazed upon Atala's countenance. Then I sprinkled the earth of sleep on her brow of eighteen springtimes and watched the features of my sister disappear gradually; I saw her graces cloaked by the curtain of eternity. Her breast for a while rose above the black soil as a white lily rises from the black sod. "Lopez," I cried out, "behold your son interring your daughter!" and I finished covering Atala with the earth of sleep.

We returned to the grotto, and I told the missionary I intended to live with him. The holy man, who knew the heart of man, guessed my thought and the turmoil of my emotions. He said to me, "Chactas, son of Out-alissi, while Atala lived, I asked you to live with me; but now your destiny is changed: you owe your life to your country. Believe me, my son, sorrows are not forever. Sooner or later they must end because the heart of man is finite. It is one of our great miseries. We cannot even be unhappy for long. Return to the Mississippi. Console your mother, who weeps for you daily and who needs your support. Be instructed in the religion of Atala when you can, and remember that you promised her to be virtuous and a Christian. I shall watch over her grave. Leave, my son. God, the soul of your sister, and the heart of your old friend will go with you."

Such were the words of the man of the rock. His authority was too great, his wisdom too profound not to obey him. The following day I left my venerable host who, in pressing me to his heart, gave me his last words, his last blessing, and his last tears. I passed by her grave. I was surprised to find there a small cross raised like a mast still visible over a shipwrecked vessel. I judged that the hermit had come to pray at the grave during the night. This mark of friendship and religion brought abundant tears to my eyes. I tried to reopen the grave, to see my beloved again. But a religious fear restrained me. I sat down on the ground newly turned. With my elbows on my knees, my head in my hands, I remained buried in bitterest reverie.

O René, it was then I made for the first time serious reflections on the vanity of our days, and even the greater vanity of our designs! My child, who has not pondered these thoughts! I am nothing more than an old stag whitened by many winters; my years quarrel with those of the crow! In spite of so many days heaped upon my head, in spite of my long experience with life, I have yet to meet the man who has not been betrayed by his phantom dreams of happiness, nor the heart which has not hidden some secret wound. The most serene heart in appearance is like the natural well of the Alachua plain: the surface is calm and pure, but when you look into its depths, a large crocodile is nourished by its waters.

Having thus seen the rising and the setting of this sun in this place of sorrow, the following day, at the stork's first cry, I readied myself to quit this hallowed sepulcher. I left it as a place from which I wished to set out in quest of virtue. Three times I invoked the soul of Atala; three times the Spirit of the Wilderness answered my cries under the funeral arch. Then I saluted the east and saw in the distance, ascending the mountain path, the hermit, who was going to the cabin of some unfortunate. Falling on my knees and embracing the grave reverently, I cried: "Sleep in peace in this foreign soil, O too unhappy maiden! For the price of your love, your exile, and your death, you will not be abandoned, even by Chactas!" Then with many tears, I left the daughter of Lopez. I fled from those woods, leaving at the foot of nature's monument a monument more august: the humble tomb of virtue.

Epilogue

Chactas, son of Outlassi, the Natchez, told this story to René, the European. Fathers have retold it to their children, and I, a wanderer in faraway lands, have faithfully reported what Indians have told to me. I saw in this recital a picture of the people as hunters, of the people as tillers of the soil; religion, first lawgiver of men; the dangers of ignorance and religious fervor, opposed to intelligence, to love, and to understanding of the true spirit of the Gospel; the struggles of passions and virtues in a simple soul; finally the triumph of Christianity over the most fiery feelings of men and their most terrible of fears—love and death.

When a Seminole told me this story, I thought it very instructive and splendidly beautiful, because he wove into it the flower of the wilderness, the charm of the cabin, and a simplicity in describing sorrow which I cannot boast that I have preserved. But one thing remained for me to know: I wondered what became of Father Aubry, and no one could tell me. I would have always remained in doubt, had not Providence, which governs all, revealed to me what I sought. This is what happened:

I had wandered the shores of the Mississippi, which once formed the southern frontiers of New France, and I was curious to see in the north another wondrous spectacle of this empire—Niagara Falls. I approached very close to the falls, in the ancient country of the Iroquois, when one morning, crossing a plain, I spied a woman seated under a tree holding in her lap a dead child. As I quietly approached the young mother I heard her say:

"If you had remained among us, dear child, how gracefully your hand would have bent the bow! Your arm would have tamed the maddened bear, and on the mountaintops your swiftness would have rivaled the racing doe. White ermine of the rocks, so young to be gone to the land of the departed! How shall you be able to live there? Your father is not there to nourish you with his hunting. You will be cold, and no one will give you skins to cover yourself. Oh! I must hasten to join you, to sing songs to you, and to give you my milk."

The young mother sang with a trembling voice; she rocked the child in her lap, wet its lips with her milk, and lavished upon her dead child all the love and affection she would have given had the child still lived.

According to the Indian custom, the woman wished to dry the body of her son among the branches of a tree, in order to take him then to the tombs of her fathers. Therefore she stripped her newly born and, breathing for a few moments into its mouth, she said: "Soul of my son, lovely soul, once your father created you with a kiss on my lips. Alas! Mine have not the power to give you a second birth!" Then she bared her breasts and hugged the icy remains, which would have been sparked to life by the fire of her motherly heart had not God reserved for Himself the breath of life.

She rose and looked about for a tree on whose branches she could cradle her child. She chose a red-flowered maple tree, festooned with garlands of apios, which gave forth the sweetest of odors. With one hand she bent a lower limb of the tree and with the other she placed the body on it. Then, her hold released, the branch returned to its normal position, bearing the remains of the innocent one, now hidden in fragrant foliage. Oh! how touching is this Indian custom! I have seen you in your lonely retreats, pompous monuments of Crassus and Caesar; but still I prefer these airy tombs of the Indian, these perfumed, flowery, verdant mausoleums, visited by the bee, rocked by balmy breezes, where the nightingale builds its nest and sings its plaintive melodies. If it be the remains of a young maiden which the hand of her lover has hung on the tree of death, or if it be the remains of a worshiped child whom a mother has placed among the nests of small birds, then the charm is redoubled.

I approached this woman who was weeping at the foot of the maple. I put my hands upon her head and cried the three cries of sorrow. Then without speaking to her, but taking a branch as she did, I scattered the insects buzzing around the child's body. I was careful not to frighten a nearby dove. The Indian spoke to it, "Dove, if you are not my child's soul which has flown away, surely you are a mother looking for something with which to build your nest. Take some of these hairs which I shall wash no more in esquine water; take some to bed your infants. May the Great Spirit preserve them for you."

Meanwhile the mother wept for joy on seeing the politeness of a stranger. As we were attending to these rites, a young man approached and said, "Daughter of Celuta, take down our child. We shall not stay here any longer. We shall leave at the first sun."

Then I said, "Brother, I wish you a blue sky, many roebucks, a beaver mantle, and hope. Are you not from this wilderness?"

"No," replied the young man, "we are exiles and are looking for a country."

As he said this, the warrior bent his head to her breast, and with the end of his bow he knocked off the head of some flowers. I perceived that there was sadness at the bottom of this story and said nothing. The woman took her son's body from the branches of the tree and gave it to her husband to carry.

Then I said, "Will you allow me to light your fire tonight?"

"We have no cabin," replied the warrior. "If you wish to follow us, we are camped on the edge of the falls."

I replied, "I would like to very much," and we set out together.

Soon we arrived at the edge of the cataract, which was announced by its loud roaring. It is formed by the Niagara River, which flows from Lake Erie and empties into Lake Ontario. Its perpendicular height is one hundred and forty-four feet. From Lake Erie to the plunge, the river races downward, and to the moment it falls, it is less a river than a sea, whose torrents hurry to the gaping mouth of the chasm. The cataract is divided into two branches and bends like a horseshoe. Between the two falls an island juts out, hollowed underneath and hanging with all its trees over this chaos of waves. The mass of the river which rushes southward rounds into a vast cylinder, then unfolds into a sheet of snow and reflects brilliant colors in the sun. The part that falls on the eastern side precipitates into a deep, gloomy chasm, like a column of water of the deluge. A thousand rainbows bend and crisscross over the abyss. Striking a fallen rock, the water rebounds in spume above whirlpools. It leaps above the forests like smoke from some vast fire. Pines, wild walnut trees, and rocks honed into fantastic shapes add to the scene. Eagles, drawn by air currents, spiral down to the depths of the chasm. Wolverines reach from the branches of low-hanging trees to snatch from the abyss the broken bodies of elk and bears.

While with awesome pleasure I contemplated this spectacle, the Indian and her husband left me. I looked for them as I followed the river above the falls, and soon I found them in a spot suitable to their mourning. They were lying on the grass with some old people, beside some human bones wrapped in animal skins. Stunned by all that I had seen in the last several hours, I sat down beside the young mother and said to her, "What is the meaning of all of this, my sister?"

She answered, "My brother, it is the earth of our country; these are the ashes of our ancestors who followed us into our exile."

"And how," I cried, "were you brought to such grief?"

The daughter of Celuta replied to me, "We are those who remain of the Natchez. After the massacre of our nation by the French to avenge their brothers, those of our brothers who escaped the conquerors found refuge among the Chickasaws, our neighbors. We remained happy with them for a long time. But it is seven months since the white men of Virginia took possession of our lands, protesting that these lands were given to them by a European king. We raised our eyes to heaven, and bearing the remains of our ancestors, we set out across the wilderness. On our journey I gave birth to my child, but since my milk was bad because of my sorrows, he died." Saying this, the young mother wiped her eyes with her tresses. I wept, too.

Soon I said, "My sister, let us adore the Great Spirit who ordains everything. We are all wanderers like our forefathers. But there is a place where we shall find repose. . . . If I did not fear having the light tongue of the white man, I would ask if you have heard of Chactas, the Natchez?"

At these words the Indian mother looked at me and said, "Who has spoken to you of Chactas, the Natchez?"

I answered, "Wisdom."

The Indian woman replied, "I shall tell you what I know because you have scattered the flies from the body of my son and because you have just spoken encouraging words about the Great Spirit. I am the daughter of the daughter of René, the European whom Chactas adopted. Chactas, who had received baptism, and René, my unhappy grandfather, perished in the massacre."

"Man goes forever from one sorrow to another," I replied, bowing my head. "Perhaps you can tell me something of Father Aubry."

"He was no more fortunate than Chactas," said the Indian woman. "The Cherokees, enemies of the French, broke into his mission; they were guided by the tolling of the bell which rang out to summon travelers. Father Aubry could have saved himself, but he did not wish to abandon his children. He remained to encourage them by his example when death would come. He was burned after being cruelly tortured. But never could they tear a cry from him which would shame his God or bring dishonor to his fatherland. During his sufferings, he did not cease to pray for his executioners nor to lament with their victims in their unhappy hour of trial. In order to wrench from him a sign of weakness, the Cherokees dragged to his feet a Christian savage whom they had horribly mutilated. But they were astonished when the young boy threw himself on his knees and kissed the wounds of the old hermit, who cried to him, 'My child, we are for a spectacle to angels and men.' The enraged Indians plunged a red-hot iron down his throat to stop his speech. Then, no longer being able to console his flock, he died.

"It is said that the Cherokees, accustomed as they were to see Indians suffer bravely, could not help admitting that there was something in the simple courage of Father Aubry which had been unknown to them and which had surpassed all earthly courage. Many among them, impressed by his death, became Christians.

"Some years later, Chactas, on his return from the white man's land, learned of the torments of the chief of prayer, and set out to gather his ashes and those of Atala. He came to the spot where the mission had been, but he could hardly recognize it. The lake had overflowed and the savannah had been changed into a swamp. The natural bridge had tumbled down and had buried under its ruins the grave of Atala and the *Groves of Death*. Chactas wandered for a long time in these parts. He visited the hermit's grotto, which he found full of brambles and raspberry bushes. A doe was suckling its fawn. He sat down on the rock that had served him for the death vigil and saw strewn about only some fallen feathers of a bird of passage. As he wept, the missionary's tame serpent came out of the near-by underbrush and coiled up at his feet. Chactas picked up this faithful friend, alone among the ruins. The son of Outalissi has related how on many occasions as night approached, he thought he

could see the shades of Atala and Father Aubry rising
from the haze of twilight. The visions filled him with a
religious terror and a sad kind of joy.

"After looking in vain for the graves of Atala and
Father Aubry, he was about to quit these parts when
the doe of the grotto began bounding in front of him.
It stopped at the foot of the mission cross. This cross
was then half-submerged in water, its wood covered
with moss, and the pelican of the wilderness liked to
perch on its worm-eaten crossbeams.

"Chactas guessed that the grateful doe had led him
to the grave of his host. He dug under the rock which
formerly had served as an altar, and there he found the
remains of a man and woman. He did not doubt that
these were the remains of the priest and the virgin,
whom the angels had perhaps buried there. He
wrapped them in bearskins, and started for his country, bearing the precious remains which rattled on his
shoulders like a quiver of death. At night, he placed
them under his head and he dreamed of love and virtue. O stranger, here you may meditate upon these
bones of Atala and Chactas himself."

As the Indian woman finished speaking, I got up. I
went to the sacred ashes and in silence I prostrated
myself. Then quickly I went away and cried, "Thus
passes on this earth all that is good, virtuous, and sen-
sitive! Man, you are but a hasty dream, a vision of sorrow; you exist only as misery; you are something only
by the sadness of your soul and the eternal melancholy
of your thought!"

I spent the night with these reflections. The following morning, at daybreak, my hosts left me. The
young warriors led the march, and the wives followed
them. The first carried the holy relics; those behind
carried their newly born. The elders made their way
slowly in the middle, placed between their ancestors

and posterity, between remembrances and hope, between the lost country and the country to come. Oh, what tears we shed when we leave our native land, when from the summit of the hill of exile, we look down for the last time upon the roofs under which we were nourished, and the river of the cabin which continues to flow sadly through the solitary fields of our native land!

Unfortunate Indians whom I have seen wander in the wilds of the New World with the ashes of your ancestors, you who have offered me your hospitality in spite of your misery—I could not return your kindness today, for I wander, like you, at the mercy of men, and less fortunate in my exile, for I do not carry with me the bones of my fathers.

RENE

Prologue

On arriving among the Natchez, René had been obliged to take a wife to conform to the Indian customs. But he did not live with her. Melancholy led him to the depths of the woods. There he spent entire days and seemed a savage among savages. Aside from Chactas, his foster father, and Father Souël, missionary at Fort Rosalie, he had given up the company of men. These two old men exercised much influence over his heart: the first by his lovable forbearance; the other, on the contrary, by his extreme severity. Since the beaver hunt when the blind sachem had told his adventures to René, René had never wanted to speak of his own. However, Chactas and the missionary desired very much to learn what sorrow had led a highly born European to the strange decision to bury himself in the wilds of Louisiana. René always proffered as reason for this reticence the insignificance of his story, "bound," he said, "by my own thoughts and feelings. As for the incident which determined me to go to

America," he added, "I must bury it in eternal oblivion."

Several years went by in this manner; the two old men could not extract from him his secret. A letter which he received from Europe, through the office of Foreign Missions, so increased his sadness that he even fled the presence of his old friends. Now they were more determined than ever to have him open his heart to them. They exercised so much tact, sweetness, and authority that finally René was constrained to satisfy their curiosity. He therefore named a day to tell them not of the adventures of his life, but of the secret feelings of his soul.

On the twenty-first of the month which the Indians call the *moon of flowers*, René went to the cabin of Chactas. He gave his arm to the sachem and led him to a sassafras tree on the bank of the Mississippi. Father Souël was not long coming to the rendezvous. Dawn was breaking. In the distance the village of Natchez could be seen, with its mulberry groves and its cabins which looked like beehives. The French colony and Fort Rosalie were visible to the right, on the bank of the river. Tents, half-constructed houses, and fortresses just begun, tracts of land being cleared by Negroes, groups of white men and Indians, presented in this small area a striking contrast of social and primitive customs. Toward the east, in the background, the sun was beginning to appear above the jagged tops of the Appalachians, which were silhouetted like azure figures against the golden expanses of the sky. In the west the Mississippi tossed its waves in widespread silence and formed for the picture a frame of indescribable majesty.

The young man and the missionary stood in raptured awe for some minutes before this beautiful picture, feeling sorry for the sachem, who could no longer enjoy it. Then Father Souël and Chactas sat down upon the grass, at the foot of the tree. René took his place in the middle, and after a moment of silence, he said the following to his friends:

"Beginning my narrative, I cannot suppress a feeling of shame. The peace in your hearts, venerable old men, and nature's calm around me make me blush for the trouble and disturbance of my soul.

"How you will pity me! How wretched will seem to you my eternal anxieties! You who have drunk all the bitter cups of life—what shall you think of a young man without fortitude and virtue who finds within himself his torments, and who can hardly weep over any misfortunes except those he has brought upon himself? Alas! Do not condemn him; he has been too much punished.

"I cost my mother her life when she brought me into the world. I was taken from her womb with irons. I had a brother whom my father favored because he saw in him his eldest son. As for me, delivered early in life to the care of strangers, I was raised far from my father's house!

"By nature I was impetuous and erratic. Sometimes disturbed and joyful, silent and sad, I gathered around me young companions. Then suddenly I would leave them and go sit by myself to gaze at the fleeting clouds, or to listen to the falling rain in the foliage.

"Each autumn I returned to my father's house, located by a lake in the middle of the forest, in a remote province.

"Timid and afraid in the presence of my father, I found ease and contentment only with my sister, Amelia. A sweet bond of temperament and tastes brought us close to each other. She was a little older than I. We loved to scale the mountainsides together, to sail on the lake, to run through the woods in autumn. Memories of these childhood adventures still fill my soul with delight. O illusions of youth and country, do you ever lose your charms?

"Sometimes we would walk in silence, listening to the gentle rustling of autumn, or to the noise of dried leaves which we dragged underfoot; sometimes, in our innocent games, we chased the swallow in the meadow or the rainbow on the rain-soaked hills; sometimes also we would whisper poetry which these spectacles of nature inspired. As a youth, I loved the company of the Muses. There is nothing more poetic, in the freshness of its passions, than the heart of sixteen. The morning of life is like the morning of day, full of pureness, imagery, and harmony.

"Sundays and holidays, I often heard through the trees in the middle of the forest the distant church bells calling the man in the fields to the temple. Leaning against the trunk of an elm, I listened in silence to this pious music. Each bronze vibration brought to my guileless soul the innocence of country living, the calm of solitude, the charm of religion, the delightful melancholy of memories of my childhood. Oh! What insensible heart has never thrilled to the sounds of bells in his native land, those bells which sang out with joy over his cradle, which announced his birth, which marked the first beat of his heart, which spread the news of his father's holy gladness and the sorrows and joys of his mother! All is contained in these delicious reveries into which we are plunged by the sound of our native bells: religion, family, country, both the cradle and the grave, both the past and future.

"It is true that Amelia and I enjoyed more than anyone else these tender, solemn reflections, because in the recesses of our hearts both of us were melancholy; we owed this to God or to our mother.

"Meanwhile my father became sick, and this illness resulted after a few days in his death. He died in my arms. I learned to know death from the lips of him who had given me life. The impression was intense; it is still vivid in my mind. It was the first time that the immortality of the soul was clearly presented before my eyes. I could not believe that this lifeless body was the author of my thoughts: I felt that it had to come from some other source, and, in my holy sorrow which approached a kind of joy, I hoped one day to join the spirit of my father.

"Another phenomenon confirmed me in this lofty idea. My father's features had assumed in the coffin something of the sublime. Why would this astonishing mystery not be an indication of our immortality? Why would all-knowing death not have engraved on the brow of her victim the secrets of another world? Why would the tomb not have some great vision of eternity?

"Amelia, overwhelmed with grief, had retired to the solitude of a tower from which she could hear, under the vaults of the Gothic château, the chanting of the priests in procession and the tolling of the funeral bells.

"I accompanied my father to his last exile. The earth closed over his remains. Eternity and oblivion pressed down upon him with all their weight, and that very evening indifferent people walked over his grave. Except for his daughter and son, it was already as if he had never been among the living.

"I had to leave my father's house, inherited by my brother. Amelia and I went to live with some old relatives.

"Stopping before the deceptive paths of life, I considered them one after the other without daring to choose. Amelia would often talk to me of the happi-

ness of the religious life; she said that I was the only
bond that kept her in the world; her eyes would gaze
at me sadly.

"With my heart moved by these pious conversa-
tions, I often directed my steps to the monastery near
my new dwelling. For a moment I was even tempted
to hide myself within its confines forever. Happy are
those who have finished their travels without leaving
port, and who have never, like René, dragged their
useless days over the earth!

"Europeans constantly in a turmoil are forced to
build their own solitudes. The more tumultuous and
noisy our hearts, the more calm and silence attract us.
These hospices of my country, opened to the wretched and weak, are often hidden in valleys, bringing to
the heart the vague feeling of sorrow and the hope of
refuge. Sometimes, too, they are found in high places
where the religious soul, like a mountain plant, seems
to rise toward heaven to offer its perfumes.

"I can still see the majestic commingling of waters
and woods around that ancient abbey where I thought
to rescue my life from the caprices of fate. I still wander at dusk in those reverberating, solitary cloisters.
When the pale moon lighted the pillars of the arcades
and sketched their shadows on the opposite wall, I
stopped to contemplate the cross that marked the
burial ground and the tall grass that grew between
the rocks around the graves. O men who have lived
far from the world and who have passed from the silence of life to the silence of death, how your tombs
filled my heart with disgust for this world!

"Whether it was my natural fickleness or a preju-
dice against monastic life, I changed my mind and decided to travel. I said good-by to my sister. She took
me in her arms with an emotion almost akin to joy, as
if she were happy because I was leaving. I could not

suppress a bitter thought about the inconstancy of human friendships.

"However, full of enthusiasm, I set out alone on the tempestuous ocean of the world, whose ports and reefs I knew not. First I visited the people who exist no more; I went and sat among the ruins of Rome and Greece: countries of strong and productive memory, where palaces are buried in the dust and the tombs of kings are hidden under the brambles. O strength of nature, and weakness of men! A blade of grass can pierce the hardest marble of these tombs, while all the dead, so powerful, shall never raise their weight!

"Sometimes a tall column stood alone in the wilderness, as a great thought stands alone in the soul which time and sorrow have crushed.

"I meditated on these monuments at every hour of the day and through all its vicissitudes. Sometimes the very sun which had shone down upon the foundations of these cities, before my very eyes, set majestically on their ruins. Sometimes the moon, rising in the pure sky between two broken funeral urns, lighted the ghostly tombs. Often, by the rays of this star which nourishes our reveries, I thought I saw the Spirit of Memory seated in deep thought by my side.

"But I wearied of searching among the graveyards, where I stirred up too often only the dust of a criminal past.

"I wanted to see if living civilizations offered more goodness and less suffering than those which had vanished. One day as I was walking in a large city, passing behind a palace, in a secluded and empty courtyard, I noticed a statue pointing to a spot made famous by a sacrifice. I was struck by the silence which reigned here. Only the wind howled about this tragic marble. Workmen were lying about indifferently at the foot of the statue or were whistling as they cut the stones.

I asked them the meaning of this statue. Some could not explain; others were completely ignorant of the catastrophe it symbolized. Nothing could better have made me realize the just measure of life's events or how little we are. What has become of these personages who were so famous? Time has taken a step and the face of the earth has been renewed.

"In my travels I especially looked for the artists and those poets who on their lyres sang of gods and of the happiness of peoples who honor laws, religion, and graves. These singers spring from a divine race. They possess the only unquestionable talent which Heaven has accorded to earth. Their life is at once innocent and sublime; they celebrate the gods with golden mouths and are the most simple of men; they speak like immortals or little children. They explain the laws of our universe, but cannot understand the most rudimentary business of life. They have marvelous ideas concerning death, and die unaware of life's meaning, like newborn infants.

"On the mountains of Caledonia, the last bard ever heard in those wilds sang to me poems whose hero was the only consolation in his old age. We were seated on four stones covered with moss; a stream trickled at our feet. In the distance a roebuck grazed among the ruins of a tower, and the wind from the sea whistled over the heather of Cona. The Christian religion, daughter of high mountains, now has planted crosses over the monuments of the heroes of Morven and played the harp of David on the banks of the same stream where Ossian once made his to sigh. As peaceful as the divinities of Selma, it now shelters flocks where Fingal once fought and has scattered angels of peace in the clouds once inhabited by murdering phantoms.

"Ancient and lovely Italy offered me its innumerable masterworks. With what reverent and poetic awe I wandered among those vast edifices consecrated to religion by the arts! What a labyrinth of columns! "What a succession of arches and vaults! How beautiful the strains of music heard around the domes, like the rolling of the ocean waves, like the murmuring of winds in the forests, or like the voice of God in His temple! The architect seems to build the poet's ideas; he makes them visible to our senses.

"And yet, what had I learned until then with so much weariness? Nothing certain among the ancients, nothing beautiful among the moderns. The past and the present are incomplete statues: one has been drawn all mutilated from the debris of ages; the other has not yet achieved the perfection of the future.

"But, perhaps, my old friends, dwellers of the wilds, are you especially surprised that, in the narration of my travels, I have not once spoken of the marvelous monuments of nature?

"One day I climbed to the summit of Etna, that volcano that burns in the middle of an island. I watched the sun rise in the immensity of the horizon above me, and Sicily was compressed like a point at my feet. The sea was rolled away into distant spaces. In this perpendicular view of the picture, rivers seemed no more than geographical lines traced on a map. But while on one side I observed these distant objects, on the other side, my eye plunged into the crater of Etna, whose fiery bowels I saw between puffs of black smoke.

"A young man full of passions, sitting at the mouth of a volcano and weeping for poor mortals whose houses he barely perceived at his feet, is surely, O elders, only an object for your pity. But whatever you may think of René, this picture offers you a glimpse of my character and of my precious existence. It is thus that, throughout my whole life, I have seen before my eyes an immense, hazy creation and a chasm yawning at my side."

After he finished these last words, René was silent, and suddenly he retreated into dreams. Father Souël gazed at him with amazement. The blind old sachem, not hearing the young man speak any more, knew not what to think of this silence.

René had fixed his eyes on a group of Indians who were gaily passing over the plain. Suddenly his countenance looked tender and tears streamed from his eyes.

"O happy savages! Why can I not enjoy the same peace that always goes with you? While I wander so fruitlessly through so many lands, you, seated quietly under your elms, let the days pass by without counting them. Needs dictate your motives and you reach better than I the goal of wisdom, like children between games and sleep. If melancholia, brought on by an excess of happiness, sometimes touches your souls, this fleeting sadness soon leaves you, and with your eyes raised to heaven, you tenderly seek for something unknown which takes pity on the poor Indian."

Here the voice of René died away again, and the young man lowered his head. Chactas extended his arm into the shadow and groped for the hand of his son: "My son, my dear son!" At the tone of his voice, the brother of Amelia came back from his dreams, and blushing for the grief he had caused, he begged his father to forgive him.

Then the old Indian spoke: "My young friend, a heart like yours cannot be calm. But control this temperament which already has heaped upon you so much grief. If you suffer more than another from the experiences of life, you must not be surprised. A great soul must bear more sorrow than a little one. Continue with your story. You have taken us through a part of Europe. Teach us now about your country. You know that I have seen France; you know how deeply attched ed I am to it. I should like to hear of the great chief, who is dead, and whose superb cabin I visited. My child, I live no more but with my memories. An old man with his memories is like a decrepit oak in our woods: it is no longer able to adorn itself with its own foliage, but must cover its nudity with strange plants that vegetate on its ancient limbs."

The brother of Amelia, calmed by these words, went on with the story of his heart.

"Alas, my father, I cannot tell you about that splendid century of which I as a child saw only the end. It was no more when I returned home. Never has a more astonishing or more sudden change taken place in a people. From the height of genius, from respect for religion, from perfection of manners, everything suddenly degenerated to wit, godlessness, and corruption.

"Thus it was in vain that I had hoped to find again in my country something to calm this raging storm within my breast, this burning desire that follows me everywhere. My study of the world had taught me nothing, and yet I had no longer sweet innocence.

"My sister, by her strange behavior, seemed to take delight in increasing my ennui. She had left Paris some days before my arrival. I wrote that I was planning to join her. But she hastened to reply that I should not, under the pretext that she did not know where her business might take her. What sad reflection did I make on friendship! When we are present, it cools; when we are absent, it vanishes; in misfortunes, it lends us no support; in times of prosperity, still less.

"Soon I found myself more alone in my native land

than I had been on foreign soil. For a time I wanted to throw myself into a kind of society which meant nothing to me and which did not understand me. My soul, which no passion had yet consumed, looked for an object on which it could lavish affection. But I noticed I was giving more than I was receiving. It was neither lofty language nor deep feeling the world was asking of me. I was busy only with shrinking my life to put it on a level with society's. Treated everywhere like an impractical dreamer, ashamed of the role I was playing, becoming more and more disgruntled with men and their petty concerns, I decided to hide away in some outlying district and to live there unknown to anyone.

"At first I was rather happy with this obscure, independent existence. Unknown, I mingled with the crowd—vast desert of men!

"Often I would sit in some rarely frequented church and spend hours in silent meditation. I watched poor old ladies prostrate themselves before the altar of the Most High and sinners kneeling in the tribunal of penance. No one left these recesses without a more serene countenance. The muffled noises from outside seemed to be waves of passion and storms of the world which came to die at the foot of the Lord's temple. O powerful God, who in secret saw me shed tears in those hallowed retreats, Thou knowest how many times I threw myself at Thy feet, begging Thee to take from me the burden of existence, or to change in me the old man! Ah, who has never felt the need to be born again, to grow young again in the waters of the spring, to dip his soul again into the fountain of life? Who has not found himself weighted down with the burden of his own corruption and incapable of doing anything great, noble, or just?

"When evening came, setting out again on the road to my retreat, I paused on the bridge to watch the sunset. Lighting up the vapors of the city, the sun seemed to be swinging slowly in a golden mist, like the pendulum of some clock of the ages. Then I fled with the night down a maze of lonely streets. Seeing the lights shining in the houses of men, I was carried away by the scenes of sorrow and joy which they provoked; I reflected that under the roofs of all those houses, I had not one friend. In the midst of my reflections, the hour tolled in measured rhythms from the tower of some Gothic cathedral. It was repeated in different tones throughout the distances from church to church. Alas, every hour in society opens a grave and makes tears to flow.

"This life, which at first delighted me, soon became intolerable to me. I wearied of the same scenes and of the same thoughts repeating themselves. I began to look into my heart, to ask myself what it was I wanted. I did not know; but suddenly I thought that the woods could be my delight. Impetuously I decided to end in a country exile a life hardly begun and in which I had already devoured centuries.

" I undertook this plan with the ardor which marked all my plans. I left at once to bury myself in some thatched hut, just as before I had left to make a tour of the world.

"People accused me of having changeable tastes, of not being able to enjoy for long the same fancy, of being the victim of an imagination which rushes precipitously to the end of pleasures, as if unable to bear their duration. They accused me of forever reaching for what I could not grasp. Alas, I only sought for some unknown good whose impulse pursues me. Is it my fault, if I find limits everywhere, if what is finite has no value to me? And yet I feel that I love the monotony of life's feelings, and, if I were still foolish enough to believe in happiness, I would seek it in habit.

"Solitude, the spectacle of nature, soon plunged me into a mood almost impossible to describe. Without parents, without friends, alone on the face of the earth, and never having been loved, I was overwhelmed by a zest for life. Sometimes I blushed suddenly and felt streams of burning lava flush my heart. Sometimes I cried for no reason, and the night was troubled by my dreams and watches. I lacked something that could fill the emptiness of my existence. I went down into the valley and climbed the mountain calling with all the strength of my desire for the ideal object of some future love. I embraced her in the winds; I thought I heard her in the moaning of the river. Everything became this imaginary phantom—the stars in the heavens and the very principle of life in the universe.

"Yet these moods of calm and agitation, of poverty and richness, were not without charm. One day I amused myself plucking the leaves from a willow and throwing them into a stream, attaching a thought to each leaf. As the current swept them away, a king who fears to lose his crown by a sudden uprising could not feel sharper pain than I as I watched each peril that threatened the debris of my branch. O the weakness of men! O the childishness of the human heart which never grows old. To what puerility our superb reason can descend! And yet, how many men attach their destiny to things as worthless as my willow leaves!

"But how can I express all the fleeting impressions I experienced on my walks? The sounds which passion makes to echo in the emptiness of a lonely heart are like the murmuring of the winds and waters heard through the silence of a plain: they delight us, but they cannot be described.

"In the midst of these uncertainties, autumn came suddenly. I entered into these months of storm with a light heart. Sometimes I would have wished to be one of those warriors wandering in the midst of winds, clouds, and phantoms; at other times I was envious of the shepherd's lot when I saw him warming his hands by the humble brushwood fire he had made in a corner of the woods. I listened to his melancholy songs, which recalled to my mind that in every country the natural song of man is sad, even when it sings of happiness. Our heart is an imperfect instrument, a lyre missing several of its strings, on which we are forced to play joyous airs in tones meant for sadness.

During the day I strayed through the heather at the edge of the forest. How little was needed to spark my dream world: a dry leaf chased by the wind before me, a cabin with smoke rising to the top of naked trees, moss trembling in the north wind on the trunk of an oak, a lonely rock, a deserted pond where the withered reed rustled! A village church tower, rising in the distance down in the valley, often caught my eye. Many times I followed the birds of passage as they flew overhead. I would imagine unknown shores, far-away climes to which they were hurrying. I wanted to be borne away on their wings. A secret thought tormented me; I felt that I was myself only a traveler, but a voice from heaven seemed to say, 'Man, the season of your migration has not yet come; wait for the wind of death to blow; then fly to those unknown shores which your heart seeks.'

" 'Rise with all speed, wished-for storms that come to bear René away into the spaces of another life!' Thus I spoke and forged ahead with great strides, my face afire, the wind whistling through my locks, feeling neither the rain nor the frost, enchanted, troubled, and like one possessed by the demon of my heart.

"At night, when the north wind shook my hut, when the torrential rains lashed upon my rooftop, when through my window I saw the moon furrow through the gathering clouds like a ghostly vessel which plows through the waves, it seemed that in the bottom of my heart life was intensified, that I had the power to create worlds. Ah! If I had only been able to share with another the transports I was experiencing! O God! If Thou hadst given me the woman of my dreams; if Thou hadst taken from my side, as Thou didst for our first father, an Eve, and led her by the hand to me . . . O Beauty celestial, I would have thrown myself at Thy feet, and embracing thee, I would have asked the Eternal God to give to you the rest of my life.

"Alas! I was alone, alone on the face of the earth! A creeping languor possessed my body. This horror of life which I had felt from childhood returned with a new potency. Soon my heart no longer nourished my thoughts, and I was aware of my existence only because of a deep-seated feeling of boredom.

"I struggled for a while against my malady, but indifferently, with no strong resolution to conquer my loneliness. At last, incapable of finding any remedy for my strangely wounded heart, which was nowhere and everywhere, I resolved to take my life.

"Priest of the Most High, who hears me, forgive a wretched soul whom Heaven had almost deprived of reason. I was surfeited with religious feeling, but I reasoned like the ungodly; my heart loved God, but my mind knew Him not. My conduct, my words, my feelings, my thoughts were only contradictions, black confusion and lies. But does man always know for what he thirsts? Is he always sure of what he thinks?

"Everything was leaving me at once: affection, the world, solitude. I tried everything and everything failed. Scorned by society, abandoned by Amelia, when solitude left me, what was there remaining? That was the last plank upon which I constructed my salvation, and I saw it tumble into the abyss!

"Having decided to rid myself of life's burden, I resolved to execute this insane crime, using the full powers of reason; nothing hurried me. I did not fix a particular moment for my death, in order to savor by long draughts the last moments of existence, in order to gather all my strength to sense my soul taking its flight, like Canus Julius.

"However, I did think it necessary to make some arrangements about my worldly possessions. I was forced to write to Amelia. I complained about her forgetfulness of me, but doubtless I allowed to pierce through some of the tenderness which overcame my heart by degrees as I wrote. Nonetheless I thought I had sufficiently concealed my secret. But my sister, accustomed as she was to probe the recesses of my soul, guessed it without difficulty. She was alarmed at the restrained tone which permeated my letter and at my questions about business affairs which had heretofore never really concerned me. Instead of answering me, she surprised me with an unexpected visit.

"To appreciate my first transports of joy upon seeing Amelia again, and later to appreciate the bitterness of my anguish, you must realize that she was the only person in the world whom I had ever loved and that all my feelings came to center themselves in her with the sweetness of my childhood memories. Therefore, I welcomed Amelia with a kind of exhilerating ecstacy. It had been such a long time since I had found someone who understood me and to whom I could lay bare my soul!

"Throwing herself into my arms, she said: 'Ungrateful you are! You want to die, and your sister lives! You suspect her heart! Don't explain, don't excuse yourself. I know everything. I have understood as if I had been with you all the while. Is it I whom you try to deceive, I who saw the first burst of emotion in your heart? Is this your unhappy character, so full of dislikes and injustices! Swear, while I press you to my heart, swear that this is the last time you will abandon yourself to your follies, take an oath never to attempt suicide.'

"As she said these words, Amelia looked at me with compassion and tenderness and covered my brow with kisses. She was almost like a mother, she was something more tender. Alas! My heart was opened again to all joys. Like a child, I asked only to be comforted and I yielded to Amelia's will. She wanted a solemn oath. I complied without hesitation, not suspecting that henceforward I could be unhappy.

"We were more than a month getting used to the delight of being together again. When, in the morning, instead of finding myself alone, I heard my sister's voice I trembled with joy and happiness. From nature Amelia had received something sublime. Her soul radiated the same innocent graces as her body, the sweetness of her feelings was infinite, and there was nothing about her mentality that was not marked by a suave and dreamy texture. One would say that her heart, her thoughts, and her voice made delightful music together. She took from woman her shyness and love, and from the angels, purity and melody.

"The moment had come when I was to expiate all my absurdities. In my delirium, I had even desired to suffer some catastrophe, so that I might at least have real reason for suffering—a dreadful wish which God, in His anger, has too well fulfilled.

"What am I about to tell you, O my friends! Look at the tears streaming from my eyes! Can I even . . .

A few days ago nothing could have dislodged this secret. . . . Now all is finished!

"Still, my friends, let this tale be buried in silence forever; remember that it has only been told under this tree in the wilderness.

"Winter was ending when I noticed that Amelia was losing something of her repose and health, at a time when she was beginning to restore my repose and health. She was becoming thinner; her eyes were hollow, her gait was listless, and her voice excited. Once I come upon her bathed in tears at the foot of a cross. The world, solitude, my presence, my absence even, the night, the day—everything alarmed her. Involuntary sighs froze on her lips. Sometimes, without tiring herself she could sustain a long walk; other times she could scarcely drag herself along. She took up tasks and left them, opened a book and could not read it, began a sentence and did not finish it. Suddenly she would burst into tears and go off by herself to pray.

"In vain I tried to fathom her dark secret. When, taking her in my arms, I questioned her, she would answer smilingly that she was like me, not knowing what was wrong with her.

"Three months passed like this, and each day she grew worse. A mysterious correspondence seemed to me to be the cause of her tears, for, depending upon the letters she received, she appeared calmer or more distraught.

"Finally, one morning, it being past our accustomed breakfast hour, I went up to her apartment. I knocked. No one answered. I opened the door and found no one in the room. I noticed on the mantel a packet addressed to me. I took it, trembling; opened it; and read this letter, which I have preserved to remove any future feeling of joy I might ever have.

"To René:

"My brother, Heaven is my witness that I would give my life a thousand times over to spare you one moment of grief. But wretched as I am, I can do nothing for your happiness. Pardon me, therefore, for leaving you like one guilty of some crime. I should never have been able to withstand your entreaties, and yet, I had to leave. . . . My God, have pity on me!

"You know, René, that I have always been inclined to the religious life. It is time that I heed Heaven's call. Why have I waited so long? God is punishing me for it. For you I had stayed in the world. . . . You must pardon me; I am very much upset by the sadness of having to leave you.

"It is now, my dear brother, that I feel the need of these retreats against which I have often heard you raise your voice. There are sorrows which separate us from men always. What would become of us unfortunate women were it not for convents? . . . I am quite convinced, dear brother, that you yourself would find much repose in these religious solitudes, for the world offers nothing which is worthy of you.

"I shall not remind you of your oath. I know the trustworthiness of your word. You have sworn it and you will live entirely for me. Is there anything more miserable than to think constantly of suicide? For a man of your nature, it is so easy to die! But believe your sister, it is more difficult to live.

"But, my brother, abandon as quickly as you can this solitude; it isn't good for you. You must seek some occupation. I know you bitterly mocked this necessity in France of *getting established*. But do not scorn so much the experience and wisdom of our elders. It is better, my dear René, to resemble common men a little and to have a little less wretchedness in your life.

"Perhaps you would find in marriage relief from your ennui. A wife and children would busy your days. And who is the woman who would not try to make you happy! The ardor of your soul, the beauty of your mind, your noble, passionate air, your proud and tender eyes—all would assure you of her love and fidelity. Ah, with what joy, she would embrace you and press you to her heart! How all her glances, all her thoughts, would be fixed upon you to shield you from the slightest pain! Before you, she would be all love and innocence; you would feel that you had found again a sister-soul. *close to nature*

"I leave for the convent of ——. This convent built by the sea suits the state of my soul. At night, from my cell, I shall hear the murmur of the waves which wash against the convent's walls; I shall think of the walks we took together through the woods, when we thought we heard sea sounds shake the tops of the pine trees. O loved companion of my childhood, shall I see you never again? Hardly older than you, I rocked you in your cradle and often we shared the same bed. Ah! If one day we might share the same tomb! But no! I must sleep alone beneath the icy marble of that sanctuary where young girls who have never loved repose eternally.

"I do not know if you shall be able to read these lines, half-stained as they are with my tears. After all, my friend, a little sooner or a little later, would we not have had to leave each other? What need have I to talk with you about the uncertainty and vanity of life? You remember young M—— who was shipwrecked off the island of Mauritius. When you received his last letter, some months after his death, his earthly remains did not even exist any more, and just when you were beginning to mourn for him in Europe, others were finishing their mourning in the Indies. What is man, therefore, the memory of whom dies so quickly? Some of his friends learn of his death when others are already consoled! Dearest René, will my memory be so promptly erased from your heart? O my brother, if I tear myself from you in time, it is only not to be separated from you in eternity.

"Amelia

"P.S. I am enclosing the deed of my worldly possessions. I hope you will not refuse this token of my affection"

"If a bolt of lightning had struck at my feet, I could not have been more shocked than I was by this letter. What secret was Amelia hiding from me? Who was forcing her to take up the religious life so suddenly? Had she restored my existence by tender affection only to forsake me impetuously? Oh, why had she come to turn me aside from my plan? A feeling of pity had brought her back to me, but soon tiring of her arduous duty, she was all too quickly abandoning her wretched brother, who had only her on the face of the earth. People imagine they have done everything when they have kept a man from death! Such were my lamentations. Then, examining the interior of my heart, I said, 'Ungrateful Amelia, if you had been in my place; if, like me, you had been lost in the emptiness of time, ah, you would not have been deserted by your brother!'

"However, when I reread the letter, I found in its lines something so sad, so tender, that all my heart melted. Suddenly flashed a thought which gave me some hope. I thought perhaps Amelia might have fallen in love with a man whom she dared not mention. This suspicion seemed to explain her melancholy, her mysterious correspondence, the passionate tone that permeated her letter. I wrote to her immediately and begged her to open her heart to me.

"It was not long before she answered me, but the letter revealed nothing about her secret. She only informed me that she had obtained dispensation from the novitiate and was about to pronounce her vows.

"I was indignant over Amelia's stubborness, over the mysteriousness of her words, and over the little confidence she placed in my affection.

"After hesitating a moment about what action I should take, I decided to go to B— to make one last effort to dissuade her. On the way, I passed the property where I had been raised. When I caught sight of the woods in which I had spent the only happy moments of my life, tears came to my eyes, and it was impossible to resist the temptation to bid them a last good-by.

"My elder brother had sold the family estate, and the new proprietor was not living there. I approached the château through a long avenue of pines. I walked across the deserted courtyards and stopped to gaze at the closed or partly broken windows, the thistle growing at the foot of the walls, the leaves strewn in the threshold of the doors, and those lonely stone steps where so often I had seen my father and his faithful servants. The steps were already covered with moss. Yellow flowers grew between the unpointed and tottering stones. An unfamiliar caretaker brusquely opened the door for me. I paused before crossing the threshold; the man said, 'Well, are you going to do exactly what that strange woman did who came here a few days ago? As she entered she fainted and I had to carry her back to her carriage.' It was easy for me to recognize the *strange woman*, who, like myself, had come back to this spot to look for tears and memories!

"I dried my eyes with my handkerchief and entered the château of my ancestors. I wandered around the rooms, where the only sound was the tapping of my footsteps. The rooms were barely lit by the faint rays which filtered through the closed shutters. I visited the room in which my mother had lost her life bringing me into the world, the room into which my father used to retreat, the room in which I had slept in my cradle, and finally the room in which my sister had received into her bosom my first vows of affection. Everywhere the rooms were stripped and spiders spun their webs in the abandoned beds. I hurried away from the château without daring to look back. How sweet, but fleeting, are the moments brothers and sisters spend together during their young years, under the care of their parents! The family of man lasts but a day. The breath of God scatters it like smoke. Hardly does the son know his father, the father his son, the brother his sister, the sister her brother! The oak tree sees its acorns germinate around it; it is not so with the children of men!

"Upon my arrival at B— I was led to the convent. I asked to speak to my sister. They told me she was not receiving anyone. I wrote to her and she replied that, since she was about to consecrate her life to God, she was not permitted to give any thought to the world, and if indeed I loved her, I would avoid heaping her with my sorrow. She added, 'However, if you plan to be present at the altar on the day of my profession, consent to serve as my father; it is the only role worthy of your courage, the only one that suits our affection and my peace of soul.'

"This cold firmness which opposed the ardor of my love threw me into a violent rage. At times I was almost on the verge of going away; at other times I wanted to remain, only to trouble the ceremony. Hell aroused in me the thought of stabbing myself in the church, and mingling my lost sighs with the vows that were tearing my sister from me. The mother superior of the convent informed me that there was a bench in the sanctuary for me, and invited me to at-echo p. 96

tend the ceremony, which was to take place on the following day.

"At daybreak, I heard the first sound of bells. . . . About ten o'clock, in a sort of agony, I took myself to the convent. Nothing can be tragic after one has been present at such a ceremony. Nothing can be sad after one has lived through it.

"A large crowd filled the church. They led me to my bench in the sanctuary, where I immediately knelt, almost oblivious of where I was or what I was doing. The priest was already at the altar. Suddenly the mysterious grille was opened, and Amelia stepped forward, adorned in all the world's finery. She looked so lovely and there shone on her face such radiance that in the church there was a stir of admiration and surprise. Overcome by the glorious sorrow of her saintly appearance, crushed by the grandeur of religion, all my designs of violence vanished. My strength left me. I felt bound by an all-powerful hand, and, instead of blasphemous threats, I found in my heart only profound reverence and humility.

"Amelia took her place under the canopy. The sacrifices began by the light of the torches, amid flowers and perfumes which rendered the holocaust charming. At the offertory, the priest took off his vestments except for a linen tunic and mounted the pulpit. In a sermon that was as simple as it was moving, he described the happiness of the virgin who consecrates herself to the Lord. As he pronounced the words: 'She appeared like the incense which is consumed in the fire,' a perfect calm and heavenly odors seemed to spread through the congregation. It was as if we were sheltered by the wings of a mystic dove, and as if angels descended upon the altar and then flew back to Heaven with perfumes and crowns.

"The priest finished his sermon, dressed again in his vestments, and went on with the sacrifice. Amelia, sustained by two young nuns, knelt on the bottom step of the altar. Then someone came to get me that I might fulfill my role as a father. At the sound of my unsteady footsteps in the sanctuary, Amelia looked as if she might faint. They stood me beside the priest to hand him the scissors. At that moment I felt my anger beginning to rise again. I was about to give vent to my fury, when Amelia, recovering her courage, looked at me so reproachfully and so sadly that I was utterly subdued. <u>Religion triumphed</u>. My sister took advantage of my distress and lowered her head. Her beautiful tresses fell to the floor under the holy scissors. A long robe of muslin replaced her worldly raiment without detracting from her beauty. The cares on her brow were hidden under a linen headband, and the mysterious veil, that twofold symbol of virginity and religion, was placed upon her shorn head. Never had she appeared so beautiful. The penitent's eyes were fixed on the dust of the world, and her soul was in heaven.

"However, Amelia had not yet pronounced her vows, and in order to die to the world, she had to pass through the tomb. My sister lay down on a marble slab. They stretched over her a pall; four torches burned at four corners. The priest, with his stole about his neck, his book in his hand, began the office of the dead, and the young virgins continued his chants. <u>O joys of religion, how magnificent you are, but how terrible too!</u> Someone had constrained me to kneel next to this mournful sepulcher. Suddenly a confused murmur came from under the shroud, and as I bowed my head, these dreadful words, heard only by myself, came to my ear. 'Merciful God, <u>let me never</u> rise from this deathbed, and <u>lavish upon my brother</u>

all Thy blessings, who has never shared my guilty passion.'

"As these words escaped from the bier, the horrible truth dawned upon me. I lost my reason and fell upon the pall. I pressed my sister in my arms, and cried out, 'Chaste bride of Christ, receive these last embraces through the chill of death and the depths of eternity, which already separate you from your brother!'

"This feeling, this cry, these tears, disrupted the ceremony. The priest stopped, the nuns closed the grille, the congregation stirred and pushed forward to the altar. They carried me away, unconscious. I was not thankful to those who revived me. Opening my eyes, I learned that the sacrifice had been consummated and my sister had been seized with a burning fever. She sent word that I should not try to see her any more. O misery of my life—a sister fearing to speak with her brother, and a brother fearing to make his voice heard by his sister! I left the convent as from a place of atonement where flames prepare us for the heavenly life, where all has been lost, as in hell, save hope.

"We can find strength of soul against a personal calamity, but to become the involuntary cause of someone else's misfortune—that is utterly unbearable. Knowing my sister's griefs, I could imagine what she must have suffered. Several things which I had been unable to understand now were explained: this mixture of joy and sadness which Amelia had felt when I was embarking upon my travels, the care she took to avoid me on my return, and this weakness which kept her for such a long time from entering the convent. Without a doubt she had thought she could cure herself. Her plans to retreat from the world, the dispensation from the novitiate, her deeding to me of all her possessions, had all apparently produced this secret correspondence which served to deceive me.

"O my friends, I knew what it was to shed tears for a hurt which was not at all imaginary! My passions, for so long vague, now with fury seized upon this new prey. I even found a kind of unexpected satisfaction in the fullness of my sorrow, and I was aware, with a secret joy, that sorrow is not a feeling which is consumed like pleasure.

"I had wanted to leave the world before the summons of the All-Powerful—that was a great sin. God had sent me Amelia both to save and to punish me. Thus, every guilty thought, every sinful act, brings in its wake disorder and sorrow. Amelia begged me to go on living. I owed it to her not to aggravate her sorrows. Besides—how strange—I had no longer any wish to die now that I was indeed wretched. My sorrow had become an occupation which filled all my waking hours; so much had my heart molded itself to ennui and misery!

"So I suddenly decided upon another course of action. I was determined to leave Europe and go to America.

"At that very moment, a fleet bound for Louisiana was being prepared in the port of B—. I made arrangements with one of the ship captains, informed Amelia of my plans, and prepared to depart.

"My sister had been at the gates of death, but God had destined for her the crown of virgins and did not wish to call her to Him so soon. Her trials on earth were prolonged. Entering for a second time into life's hard course, the heroine, bent under the cross, went forward courageously meet her afflictions. She saw only final victory in the fight, and in overwhelming difficulties, only overwhelming glory.

"The sale to my brother of the little property I had, the long preparations of the convoy, and unfavorable winds kept me for a long while in port. Each morning I would go seeking news of Amelia. Always I would return with new reasons to admire and weep.

"I made endless foot excursions around the convent on the edge of the sea. I would often notice, in a little grilled window which overlooked a deserted beach, a nun seated in a thoughtful posture. She was contemplating some aspect of the ocean where some vessel could be seen sailing to the ends of the earth. Several times, in the moonlight, I saw again the same nun at the bars of the same window. She was meditating upon the sea lighted by the night star. She seemed listening to the noise of the waves as they broke sadly on the solitary beaches. *echo!*

"I can still hear the bell which during the night called the nuns to their watches and prayers. As it chimed solemnly, and the virgins approached silently the altar of the All-Powerful, I would run to the convent. There, alone under the walls, I listened in reverent ecstasy to the mournful tones of the hymns as they blended under the vaults of the temple with the gentle music of the waves.

"I do not know how all these things, which should have nourished my anguish, instead dulled the pain. My tears were less bitter when I shed them on the rock in the winds. Even my sorrow, by nature excessive, bore with it some remedy. We enjoy what is uncommon, even when it is a calamity. I almost conceived the hope that my sister would also become less miserable.

"A letter which I received from her before my departure seemed to confirm my notions. Amelia pitied me tenderly because of my sorrow and assured me that time would heal her wounds. 'I have not despaired of happiness,' she wrote to me. 'The very excess of my sacrifice, now that it is consummated, brings some repose. The simplicity of my companions, the purity of their vows, the regularity of their lives, everything mantles my days with balm. When I hear the roaring storms and the sea bird comes to beat its wings on my window, I, poor dove of heaven, think of the happiness of finding shelter from the tempest. The holy mountain is here; here is the lofty summit where we can hear the last noises of the world and the first movement of Heaven's overture. It is here that religion beguiles a gentle soul. For the most violent love, religion substitutes a kind of burning chastity in which lover and virgin find fulfillment. It purifies our sighs and transforms into an eternal flame what was perishable. It blends its divine calm and innocence with the remains of anguish and voluptuousness in a heart which seeks rest and in a life which seeks apartness.'

"I do not know what Heaven has set aside for me or whether it wished to warn me that storms would follow me everywhere. The order was given to the fleet to depart; already several ships had weighed anchor at sunset. I made arrangements to spend the last night on land, that I might write my letter of farewell to Amelia. Toward midnight, I applied myself to the letter. Tears moistened my paper. The winds howled. I listened. In the midst of the storm I could make out cannon shots of alarm mixed with the knelling of the convent bells. I sped to the sea's edge, where all was deserted and where was heard only the breaking of the waves. I sat on a rock. On one side spread before me the glittering waves; on the other side the somber walls of the convent lost themselves in the reaches of the heavens. A dim light appeared at the grilled window. Was it you, O my Amelia, who, prostrated at the foot of a crucifix, was beseeching the God of Storms to spare your unhappy brother? Storm on the waves, calm in your retreat; men broken on reefs at the very entrance to an untroubled refuge; infinity on the other side of the cell wall; the moving beacon lights for ships, the motionless light of the convent; the incertitude of the navigator's destiny, the vestal virgin knowing in a single day all the future days of her life; and yet, a soul such as yours, Amelia, stormy like the ocean; a shipwreck more terrible than the mariner's— the whole picture is still indelibly traced in my memory. Sun of this new sky now a witness of my tears, echo of American shores repeating René's accents, it was on the morrow of this terrible night that, standing on my ship's forecastle, I watched my native land disappear in the distance forever. Long it was that I watched the last swaying of the trees on the coast of my country, and the roofs of the convent that were sinking below the horizon."

As René finished his narration, he drew a piece of paper from his breast pocket and gave it to Father Souël. Then throwing himself into the arms of Chactas, and holding back his sobs, he gave the missionary time to peruse the letter which had just been put into his hands.

It was from the mother superior of— and described the last moments of Sister Amelia of Mercy, now dead, a victim of her zeal and charity, while caring for her companions stricken by a contagious disease. The whole community was inconsolable, and they looked upon Amelia as a saint. The mother superior added that, for the thirty years she had been head of the house, she had never seen a nun whose disposition was as gentle and placid, nor a nun who was more happy to quit life's tribulations.

Chactas took René into his arms. The old man wept bitter tears. "My child," he said to his son, "would that Father Aubry were here. He could draw from the depths of his heart a certain peace which, while calming them, did not seem strange to the storms. He was the moon on a tempestuous night; the roving clouds could not bear it along on their course; pure and unalterable, it raced calmly above them. Alas, for me, everything disturbs and carries me away!"

Till then Father Souël had said nothing, but had listened gravely to René's story. Deep within, his heart was tender; outwardly he was uncompromising. The sachem's sensitivity forced him to break silence.

"Nothing," said Father Souël to the brother of Amelia, "nothing in this story merits the pity which is shown to you here. I see a young man intoxicated with his illusions, displeased with everything, withdrawn from the burdens of society, given to idle dreams. One is not, sir, a superior man because he sees the world in shadow. A man who hates his fellow men and life has no breadth of vision. Look further into the distance and you shall soon be convinced that all the evils of which you complain are nothing. But what a shame not to be able to see the real misfortune of your life without being obliged to blush! All the purity, all the goodness, all the faith, all the saintly crowns, can scarcely tolerate the very idea of your sorrows. Your sister has atoned for her sin; but, if I must have my say, I fear that, through a terrible injustice, a confession coming from the depths of the tomb has troubled your soul. What do you do all alone in the forests, where you waste your days, neglecting all your duties? Saints, will you say to me, are buried away in the deserts? But they were there weeping, extinguishing the fires of their passions while you were, it seems, igniting yours. O young presumptuous one, you have believed

man is sufficient unto himself. <u>Solitude is evil for
him who does not live with God!</u> It doubles the soul's
power; at the same time, it takes from man the op-
portunity to exert himself. Whoever has received
talents should use them in the service of his fellow
creatures. If he leaves them unused, he is first punished
by conscience, and sooner or later Heaven chastises
him."

Disturbed by these words, René raised his head
from the bosom of Chactas. The blind sachem began
to smile, and this smile of his lips, which did not match
the expression of his eyes, had some mysterious heavenly quality. "My son," said the aged lover of Atala,
"he reproaches us severely; he is correcting both the
old and the young man, and he is right. <u>Yes, you must
give up this strange life which is full only of woes.
There is happiness only along common paths.</u>

"One day the Mississippi, still rather close to its
source, tired of being only a limpid stream, called
snows from the mountains, waters from other streams,
rains from the tempests. It overflowed its banks and
ravaged its lovely shores. The proud stream at first
applauded its power. But, seeing that everything became desert by its passage, as it flowed along abandoned in solitude, its waters always troubled, it longed
for the humble bed which nature had dug for it. It
longed for the birds, the flowers, the trees, and the
brooks, erstwhile modest companions of its peaceful
course."

Chactas stopped speaking, and the voice of the
flamingo, hidden in the reeds of the Mississippi, announced a storm for the middle of the day. The three
friends started back to their cabins. René walked along
in silence between the priest, who was praying, and
the blind sachem, who groped his way.

It is said that, encouraged by the two old men, he returned to his wife, but found no happiness. He died a short time afterward with Chactas and Father Souël, in the massacres of the French and Natchez in Louisiana. The rock is still pointed out where he went to sit and gaze at the fires of sunset.